Irina Muravyova, born in 1952 in Mo... philologist by training. She is a Pushkin scholar and translates poetry from English and German.

In 1985 she emigrated to the USA and currently lives in Boston where she lectures at Harvard and edits the *Boston Marathon*, a Russian-language literary gazette.

She has two books of prose to her credit: *The Nomadic Soul* (Terra Publishers, Moscow, 1992) and *The Curly-headed Lieutenant* (Hermitage Publishers, USA, 1995). Many of her stories have been published in Russia's best literary journals.

Irina Muravyova is one of the finest Russian women authors today. Her prose is poetic and precise, always on the lookout for the precious grains of love and kindness in a hostile world.

'Her prose tends to poetry, it is marked with dignity and faith in her unfortunate homeland.'

— *Russkaya Mysl*

'...an aspiring talent emerging from the recent group of emigre Russian writers.'

— *World Literature Today*

'We are proud to present the Russian author Irina Muravyova, whose stories show what powers women may call on in order to survive.'

— From the introduction to the *Women on the Case* (26 original stories by the best women writers of our time)

# Glas New Russian Writing

a book series of contemporary Russian writing
in  English translation
edited by Natasha Perova & Arch Tait

VOLUME 22

# Irina Muravyova

# The Nomadic Soul

Translated by John Dewey

GLAS Publishers (Russia)
Moscow 119517, P.O.Box 47, Russia
Tel./Fax: +7(095)441 9157
E-mail: perova@glas.msk.su

GLAS Publishers (UK)
Dept. of Russian Literature,
University of Birmingham, Birmingham, B15 2TT, UK
Tel/Fax: +44(0)121-414 6047
E-mail: a.l.tait@bham.ac.uk

WORLD WIDE WEB: http://www.bham.ac.uk/glas

USA and Canada:
Ivan R. Dee
1332 North Halsted St., Chicago, Illinois 60622-2694, USA
Tel: 1-312-787 6262; Fax: 1-312-787 6269
Toll-free: +1-800-462-6420
E-mail: elephant@ivanrdee.com

Contributing editor: Joanne Turnbull
Camera-ready copy: Tatiana Shaposhnikova
Front cover: Detail from Alexander Deineka's 'A Parisienne'

GLAS GRATEFULLY ACKNOWLEDGES THE SUPPORT OF THE SWEDISH
PEN AND DR MARION GRAFIN DONHOLL OF DIE ZEIT

ISBN 5-7172-0048-X

Printed at the 'Novosti' printing press, Moscow

1004114298T

# CONTENTS

*To the memory of my beloved friend Tanya Fradkina*

# The
# Nomadic
# Soul

# PART ONE

*T*he beach at Lynn was empty, apart from some seagulls dotted about the smooth sands. There was a smell of rotting seaweed.

How had I come to be here? Quite simply: by driving half an hour from Boston.

But seriously: what was I doing here? What chance wind had brought me to this provincial American seaside town with its clapboard houses, and to Rabbi Zaychik's synagogue?

There was a concert taking place in the synagogue. It was rather stuffy in there, with stout Russian ladies sweltering in their best frocks. A boy of about seventeen was singing a romance to words by Sasha Chorny, clenching his fists with the effort as he intoned in an unsteady bass voice:

> *Sleep, my son, your Mummy's gone —*
> *Gone to Paris, little one...*

Stop! Who was this Mummy? Why Paris? And why did it all sound so strangely familiar — as if at some time I myself had been that tearful mother abandoning her curly-haired child to run off to Paris with her lover? No, don't call him that. But what, then? What was he? Could you really say he was everything in the world to her? What about that boy (christened Nikolay, but known in the family as Koko) — that boy with the fair eyelashes whose piercing cries of 'Mummy!' rang through the house every morning: wasn't he everything in the world to me?

But what have I got to do with all this this, for heaven's sake? It was another woman, do you hear — another woman who hastily gathered together a few essential items and, her face red with the effort, fastened all eleven buttons up the back of her grey travelling dress. It was she, not I, who went into the darkened nursery, bent over the cot, kissed that little face redolent of milk and made the sign of the cross over it, then closed behind her the front door of the large detached house in the Arbat that was her home.

Yet the day before... Yes, it was only the day before that they had lingered in his study with its leather upholstery and odours of stale tobacco. Outside the windows a heavy May downpour was in full spate, breaking off twigs of lilac. She was sitting on the sofa, while he stood with his back against the glass doors of a bookcase and its colourful array of bindings. His face was white and quivering, his eyes wild.

'I ask only one thing: that we keep up the appearances of marital life, so that our child can grow up in a normal family, so that he...'

Perhaps it was me after all? Perhaps it was me, shielded from the cold May rain by the walls of that house in the Arbat?

At that moment I felt nothing but detestation for his voice, for that hand with its thin wedding ring; yet I understood that they would always be with me, that I should never manage to...

'Let me go. I'll come back in a month. One month, that's all. You yourself suggested we keep up appearances, and I shall do that, I promise. But now that we've finally clarified matters... Just one month, I beg you...'

'Very well. He won't notice anything, he can stay at the dacha with my sisters and his nanny. You can go — and may God above be your judge!' There was a dull glint from his wedding ring as he gestured with his hand towards the ceiling.

The heavens showed no sign of themselves. Outside the window there was no sky at all, just rain pouring down: driving rain that filled the city with the fresh, heady fragrance of grass.

It was dry in Paris, though. Our hotel room smelled of lavender. The warmth of our hands was held by the lavender-scented soap as it slowly dried out. For the first time I woke up next to someone who for me was... what? That boy with the fair eyelashes — the curly-headed boy whose penetrating cry of 'Mummy!' rang through the house every morning — wasn't he everything in the world to me?

What chance wind took her there? Most likely the same wind which brought me today to this stuffy synagogue in the seaside resort of Lynn and, puffing out its white fluffy cheeks, deposited me on a chair next to a stout lady sweltering in her best frock. Soul drifting freely through ethereal mists, today belonging to me and beating your tiny wings so painfully against my ribs, but yesterday assigned to her who stood unmoving in the doorway of that house in the Arbat: who would be so rash as to say what wind bears you, my free, tearful soul, through a world startled into wariness as you brush against it on your passage, seeking, like a shadow cast on water, your own time and space?

\* \* \*

'...No-one else might notice it, but I say there's an incredible likeness there. Of course, Lydia was pretty as a picture, whereas this one has her father's features, more's the pity. But her smile, her mannerisms! And her eyes! Just like her! I even find it unnerving sometimes, the way she fiddles with her plait when she gets worked up. Exactly the same gesture! How do you explain that? You could understand if she were her granddaughter, then at least she'd be directly related, wouldn't she? But Lydia was... what, her great-aunt.'

'Did Lydia die in Paris, then?'

'No, what gave you that idea? She came back just before the war broke out. She'd dragged out that month she promised to come back after. Of course, she must have taken leave of her senses, leaving her husband and running off with a lover like that. Like in some cheap novelette! Not that there was anything the least bit bohemian about her, mind you — she was more your conventional housewife, your home-loving type... She was just so besotted she couldn't think straight any more. And then there was that idiotic obsession with truthfulness that she had! How many women are unfaithful to their husbands, but keep quiet about it? But she wasn't like that... Still, what else would you expect from someone educated at the Smolny Institute? *La crème de la crème*, they were. As for that drip she ran off with, I can't to this day imagine where she could have picked him up. How could she, with her upbringing, consort with him openly like that, with the whole city looking on? And then Paris... That was all her idea, you know: he wasn't to blame at all, poor fellow. Do you think he wanted to come between her and her husband? Do you think he wanted to shoulder all that burden? As for her, she couldn't take it — cracked up, she did. No, I often think to myself: God forbid that my girl should ever suffer a fate like hers! And that likeness to her is something we could well do without.'

'Oh, come on — outward likeness can be a matter of pure chance!'

'What are you saying, Anya? In that case everything in the world could be pure chance, ourselves included. Tell me: isn't marriage a matter of pure chance, then?'

'It depends which marriage you're talking about...'

'I'm talking about any marriage, for heaven's sake! You remember how close my husband and I were for all those years? But then if you look at it like that, our marriage really does seem to have happened purely by chance...'

\* \* \*

She was still in Paris, although she should long since have returned to Moscow, where the man with the plump white face sat for hours at a time in the darkened nursery, his eyes, reddened by sleepless nights, fixed on that little face redolent of milk. She should long since have returned to Russia, where following on from the rain, powdery snow had whitened houses and fences in the space of a day, and where now a cab encrusted with icy flakes drove up through this first snow to halt outside a corner house on Bolshaya Dvoryanskaya Street.

'Liza, come quickly and look, Mr Lopukhov's just arrived! The barrister I told you about, do you remember? The one who was at the Aseyevs' last summer? From St Petersburg? He's setting up in legal practice here, you know — his estate's about fifteen miles from Mummy's. Come here, Liza!'

She went over to the window, hunching her thin shoulders.

She had a black ribbon tied in her plait and was wearing a blue and white plaid dress. Her hair, she herself had to admit, was thin and nothing special to look at — pigtails. Now Lydia's hair — that was something different! Lydia was in Paris, for heaven's sake. Was she out of her mind? Mummy and Daddy had been talking about her again yesterday, and Mummy had been crying. Last month Daddy had been to Moscow and seen Nikolay Vasilyevich and Koko, and he'd brought back some photographs: Koko sitting sad-eyed on a little white horse. Lydia must have been out of her mind. So that was Lopukhov, was it? He was settling up with the cab driver. Quite a young-looking face, he had. His moustache gleamed silver, as if powdered. Now he'd grabbed his bag and bounded up the steps to the front door. What was he so full of beans about?

All the following day in class she was absent-minded, as if in a dream. Fat Nadya Subbotina handed her a little album bound in velvet. It was the leavers' class, and they were all writing each other little mementos in verse. Nadya Subbotina had no plans to enrol for women's higher education: she was going to marry her cousin. They'd applied to the Synod for a special dispensation, which had been granted. What an idiot Subbotina was! She'd get married, have children and spend all her time quarrelling with the cook. That wasn't for Liza: in August she, Lala and Musya would be off on the train to Moscow — off to the women's French course in Moscow! Off to hear Shalyapin! Blok, Bely and Severyanin were all there. Lydia had told her all about it. *Three Sisters* at the Moscow Art Theatre! No-one would even suspect that she came from the provinces. As for that Lopukhov, there was nothing special about him. Musya said he was a hard drinker, and that he

gambled at cards. And she said he went out to the gypsy camp to
hear the gypsies sing. Well, Daddy used to do that when he was
young, but Musya said Lopukhov had a gypsy woman as his
mistress. He sounded just like the character in that story by
Tolstoy, *A Living Corpse*!

'Write something,' said Subbotina, indicating the album with
her eyes. What an idiot she was! Every last space in her album
taken up, yet still she wanted more. God, who'd come up with
this priceless gem?

> When the earth in evening's shade is lurking,
> I'll wait for my doorbell to give voice.
> Dear friend, your duty you'll be shirking
> If to visit me then is not your choice.

She turned the page to avoid being contaminated by such
drivel and wrote out in a sloping hand:

> My soul is like a nest where, fluttering
> And struggling to be free, young fledglings sing, —
> But, when the last of these has learned to fly,
> Will be to an abandoned house akin,
> With doors ajar, through which the autumn sky
> Sends the first snow, and fallen leaves drift in.

Odd that this poem of Alexander's should have lodged so
firmly in her memory. He'd given it to her last summer at their
dacha: taken it out of his waistcoat pocket and presented it to her.
That morning they'd picked water-lilies at Chudin Pond. There'd
been a lot of people there, but only one rowing boat, and that
was leaky. Alexander had been invited to stay with them by her
brother, Sasha. In her mind she conjured up a picture of her
brother: thin, stooping, with long arms, and wearing the uniform

of a railway engineering student. One couldn't even say he looked all that young. In fact, for a twenty-four-year-old his face didn't look young at all, with its sallow complexion and enormous bulging eyes. He'd contracted tuberculosis as a child, and Mummy (who had just buried her eldest daughter — another Lydia, after whom our Lydia was named) had dropped everything and whisked him off to various health spas for a year. She'd put him on a diet of fresh German milk straight from the cow, pumped him full of sea air, and nursed him through it. Even so he'd continued to suffer poor health. The slightest thing would bring on a feverish chill. How on earth did he cope with studying in St Petersburg, built on those marshes? Nanny always said, 'Children bring their parents nothing but woe,' and she was right. Sasha coughing, Lydia in Paris... What did all that do to Mummy? Oh, if it weren't for the French course she wouldn't leave her for anything in the world, she'd never go to Moscow! After all, she could get married too if she wanted, to Alexander. For hadn't he fallen in love with her then, after the water-lilies? 'He's handsome, a real Prince Charming,' Nanny had said. A prince he might be, yet he'd blushed to the roots of his hair when he'd given her that poem! He hadn't said anything about being in love, though. Only before he was due to leave had he knocked at the door of her room, his jacket buttoned up, his hair neatly parted and gleaming.

'I do not venture to ask for your hand in marriage, Liza,' he'd said to her, 'for I know I should be refused. Yet permit me, as they say in uplifting books, to hope. Permit me to wait.'

And he'd kissed her hand, elegantly and with old-world gallantry. That evening, unable to keep it to herself, she'd told her mother all about it. Her mother had laughed at first, but then she'd looked sad. Of course, she'd remembered Lydia. Most of her thoughts revolved around Lydia these days.

It was really embarrassing having to walk around with a satchel on her back like some little schoolkid. She was grown-up now, a young lady, soon to be a student on a women's higher education course. But Mummy didn't want her to develop a stoop like Sasha and wouldn't let her carry a bag.

He came out of his front door just as she was approaching hers on the opposite side. The street was empty, and sparse flakes of dry snow fluttered in the bright sunlight. He paused for an instant, glancing at her absent-mindedly. Their eyes met. There was nothing special about him. Lopukhov by name, Lopukhov by nature, she thought.* He smiled as he pulled his gloves on. She frowned, unable to decide whether he'd smiled at her or not, and stood watching him go with her mouth half-open, quite forgetting that this was not at all the done thing for a grown-up young lady, soon to be a student. Her shoulders were aching from the satchel. He had set off down the road at a brisk pace, almost running, with flakes of dry snow settling on his back as he went.

\* \* \*

'...I have a craven fear of returning home, even though thoughts of Koko torment me more than ever. If you can, Mummy, if I may ask your forbearance at least in this, then do not condemn me. The thought that my whole life is finished fills me with horror. I have recurring dreams about locked gates: I have only to fall asleep to see them in front of me. Nikolay Vasilyevich would take me back at once, but the very thought of

---

*The word "lopukh" used colloquially means "simpleton." (*Transl.*)

resuming our senseless life together throws me into despair. I know what you will think when you read this letter, Mummy dear: you will think of my selfishness, my terrible self-absorption, and no doubt you will be right. Otherwise, would all this have happened? However that may be, I hope that my health will recover, and that three months from now I shall embrace you all again, and that you will find it in your heart to forgive me...'

\* \* \*

I returned to Moscow just before the outbreak of war. By a strange coincidence it was pouring rain. Rivulets ran down the dark-green signboard with its black lettering: Dr N.V. Filitsyn. Nervous and psychiatric disorders. The front door opened, and someone came out, putting up a silk umbrella as he went on his way. My legs felt like jelly as I stepped forwards, out of the rain and into the darkened hallway.

He was standing in the doorway of his study, not looking at me.

Stop! What is this? I'm getting confused here. What have I got to do with it? I'm sitting in this synagogue in the provincial seaside resort of Lynn, brought here by a wind that puffed up its white cheeks and blew, drying my grey travelling dress on the way.

How many years have gone by... No wonder it's dry...

She removed her hat and sank down on a chair. Neither of them said anything for a while, and he did not look at her.

'Where's Koko?'

He did not turn his head or alter the direction of his rigid gaze.

'I said, where's Koko?' she repeated in a faint voice, frightened now.

'Koko's with his aunts,' he replied calmly. 'They're bringing him here tomorrow. I thought it would be better for us to discuss matters in his absence.'

'I'm not prepared to discuss anything, I've just come back to be with Koko. I can't imagine how we're going to sort things out between us, because...'

'Because you persist in being another man's mistress!' he suddenly yelled, fixing his bloodshot eyes on her face. 'How I hate you! Yes, I hate you,' he repeated in a loud whisper, savouring the words. 'You have no right to return to this house, you have no right to touch our child with hands that have touched... How I hate you!'

'Then why did you allow me to return?' she whispered.

'Why? Because I love him, because he is everything to me! I have nothing, nobody apart from him. If it weren't for him I should have strung myself up long before now. Yes, strung myself up from the nearest hook, without a second thought! He may be only six years old, but he understands everything, everything! Only he can reconcile me to this sordid life. And you're his mother, more's the pity for him and me. Do you really think I could deprive him of his mother, of what is his by right? Just the fact of asking why I allowed you to return shows your complete and utter lack of understanding!'

'What do you want me to do now, then?' she asked quietly. 'Wait, don't shout at me — for the sake of all that's holy, don't shout at me, hear me out. The fact is, I'm not well, there's something wrong with my heart. Let me finish! I don't ask for pity of any kind, because in this terrible mess we're in you will always be in the right and I shall be the guilty party, but I...'

'I don't give a damn for your ailments! Not a damn, do you hear? I prayed to God to send you at least some punishment for all we've been through, for all that my son has had to suffer in his poor little heart!'

'Very well, I shall say no more. Even if you wish me dead...'

'I don't wish you dead. I don't wish anything for you, it's all a matter of complete indifference to me. You can stay here as lady of the house, in full charge of domestic arrangements. I'm well aware that your inborn depravity gives you no choice but to continue with this sordid liaison or even seek out some new one. You're no more to blame for your proclivities than my patients for their hallucinations and obsessions. Your psyche has just become enslaved by the flesh: it's not uncommon. I even feel sorry for you, if that makes you feel any better...'

My arms and legs had gone dead. All I could feel was this bird fluttering in my throat, constantly struggling to spread its wings and escape, and so allow me to draw breath. But its wings wouldn't spread, and I couldn't get any air...

...and then came her automatic response, filling the silence that had fallen in the hallway: 'What proclivities? Why do you have to insult me like that?'

'My God, you're so naive I could laugh!' he said, and gave a rapid burst of laughter. 'Can't you see what I'm talking about —

what I became aware of during the very first months of our married life? You were still practically a child, but I saw through you completely! You never loved me, you were as cold as a fish towards me, and yet your instinctive depravity gave birth to this quite outstanding artistry, this awful seductive allure — even in your relations with me, for whom you had no feelings of love! Do you think I don't remember the way you used to smile at me at nights? You even contrived to turn your pregnancy into a kind of display. In the final month, when you started to walk with that duck-like waddle, you even managed to flaunt that in such a way as to make everyone ogle you and your body!'

'I feel unwell. I shall go to my room if you have no objection.'

'You do that.' And with a cough he made way to let her pass.

The sun lay like a delicate fan, red and low in the sky, on Bolshaya Dvoryanskaya Street. He closed the door behind his last client. That was it for today. He stretched until his joints clicked and went over to the window. A cab had drawn up outside the house opposite, and he recognized the girl (really quite a young lady now) with a black ribbon in her hair who jumped down from the cab. A young woman in a light-blue striped dress and a boy of about seven in a traditional sailor suit stepped down after her on to the dusty dry pavement. As they stopped at the door, the woman clutched at her heart. The girl with the ribbon tugged at the bell-pull for all she was worth, and the door was thrown open. Behind the full figure of the housemaid he could make out the dark-eyed girl's parents, with whom he already had a nodding acquaintance as neighbours. The two of them ran out together to the woman, who was still clutching her heart, and supported her from either side. He caught a snatch of their distraught conversation, something like: '...didn't let us know... why not...' and then the door was slammed shut. He guessed this was the elder daughter who had caused a scandal by going off to Paris and had now presumably returned. The boy in the sailor suit would be her son. He hadn't managed to catch a glimpse of her face beneath the dark-blue hat, but was struck by her gesture of clutching at her heart in that way. It suddenly occurred to him that life still had genuine feelings to offer. Pain, love... Who knows... Love, he thought, not that animal passion he had known with Tanya, from which even now a certain irritated bitterness remained in his heart. Why didn't he just chuck it all in here and leave? No, that wasn't on: the practice was doing quite well, and he needed the money. Still, he could wait a bit, get his sisters set up and see his mother right, and then chuck it all in, and good riddance. He could go to Paris, too. Freedom! Yet he knew he wouldn't do it. He was only too aware of his own penchant for compromise, which paralyzed the will and sustained in him a certain outward well-being that was in constant danger of collapse. He went over to the sideboard and poured himself a glass of vodka. 'I shall be driven to drink through sheer boredom in this hole yet,' he thought, although he knew it was not true. A saying of Pushkin's suddenly surfaced in his memory: 'Boredom is part of the baggage of any rational being.' What a curse to be well-read! Whatever thoughts you might have, they'd already been expressed by somebody else before you! You ended up recalling other people's words as a kind of substitute for your own life. And when would his life begin, if ever? His head had started spinning slightly from drinking the vodka on an empty stomach, and he made an effort to hold on to his train of thought. Although it was certainly true that he'd never denied himself all that much, all the same life left him with a monotonously aching sensation, as of water flowing past just out of reach of his parched mouth. Tanya had been the only drop to fall directly on his lips. She had moistened them, but without quenching his thirst. He had just been stronger than the passion, that was all, more rational, and this had stopped him from taking the decisive step. He knew that he often gambled against fate and tried to outsmart it, but that fate always won out in the end, forcing him to pay dearly for his own cleverness. What other explanation could there be for this emptiness, this oppressive sense of irritation? Best to shut himself in his office here and read Plutarch. It would be quiet and peaceful. The ancients had understood the nature of things more clearly, had been closer to the truth. Living in St Petersburg had opened his eyes a lot: he'd seen the emptiness of it all, the pettiness. How unaware they all were of their own blinkered view of things, their obsession with ephemera! Why were none of them nauseated by all the endless posing? If there was one sickness from which Russia suffered above all, it was the sense of its own dramatic exclusivity. Every drunken lout got a kick out of beating his chest and shouting exultantly: 'Yes sir, I'm a Russian!' So what, one asked oneself. Perhaps it was the overblown size of the country itself that aroused in them this perverse sense of their own significance? Yet in spite of everything he felt sorry for them. None of them knew peace of mind, none of them was happy. Any encounter with human stupidity had always left him with a sharp sense of despair. As a student he had taken a passing interest in politics and attended the meetings of a political discussion group for a while. But there he had come across such opinionated stupidity, hardly excusable even on the grounds of youth, that he had stopped going soon enough. He had sensed in his own mind that politics and talking were one thing, and human life something else completely. There was something in the nature of an unthinking game in this universal passion for politics. No, none of that was for him. Best to shut himself in his office here, say good riddance to everything and read Plutarch.

\* \* \*

Wait, rest for a while. Soon the war will begin, followed by the revolution; the world of my house will collapse, and I shall have to write of people forced to grow up too soon, of hunger and death. I shall have to feel for myself my family's weak roots being loosened from the churned-up soil, then dried by a searing wind until they wilt and crumble, before finally being torn from the soil for ever.

I am sitting on the short green grass of a vacant lot in the centre of Boston, surrounded by an ever-shifting mesh of loud American speech. Immediately in front of me a long crocodile of black children stretches across the dappled green. So that none of them get lost, the children are all rather comically linked together by one piece of string, one end of which is held by a tall, long-legged black woman. A shaggy dog with pointed ears lies down next to me on the grass. Saliva drips from its mouth: it is hot. As if on command the children turn their round, close-cropped black heads. 'Hi, doggy!' they say amiably. The long-legged black woman tugs at the string. 'Come on, kids!' she calls, and the meek children with large heads and bright eyes quickly and obediently fall back in line. I watch this long black centipede in sandals of various colours mount the slope, twisting its round heads this way and that, and, linked by the piece of string, cross the road...

Through ethereal mists, across wide blue expanses, borne on the white wind, by the power of blood, without stirring, without changing position on the Boston grass, I return to my own soil, my own land.

\* \* \*

'Of course we ought to get divorced, Mummy — it's the only thing to do, because it's wrong to live the way we are now! But how could we get divorced? What would we do with Koko?'

Her hair had fallen down over her eyes. She was sitting at the foot of her mother's bed, shielding her face from the night-light with outspread fingers. Although it was almost dark in the room, she found even this light disconcerting and kept her head lowered so that it was screened by her hair. Her fingers, lit lemon-yellow from behind by the flame, were trembling.

'My God, what on earth am I going to do?'

'Lydia,' said her mother quietly, cautiously trying to look into her face, 'what about that man? Your...'

'Mummy!' She let her hand fall on the bedcover and threw her head back sharply. 'Mummy, he's got nothing to do with all this. He has his life, and I have mine, and I don't expect anything of him, anything at all. This whole thing is a cross I have to bear, do you understand? It's a cross, not a source of strength.'

'But he does... and don't get angry, now, I just want to understand: he does love you, doesn't he?'

'Mummy, you're talking like a child! What does that mean:

loves me? Does he love me, does he not, will he kiss me, will he not? Yes, he loves me, but those months in Paris when I was ill were absolute hell for him — because of the commitment, because I seemed to be forcing him into a decision for which he was completely and utterly unprepared. He has his own family, for heaven's sake — he still cares for them, and he's living with them again, after all that's happened. After everything we've been through he's gone back to his wife, just as I've gone back to Nikolay Vasilyevich! Only when I think about it all, I'm filled with such horror I can't even breathe. I just want to pinch myself hard and wake up — although in fact I haven't been sleeping properly at all, I've been taking sedatives for a long time. I just wish I could wake up and find it's all gone away, and there's just you, and Koko... Dear God! As for him, I don't even know what he feels... We don't even talk about it, as if it were somehow not the done thing...'

She wept, sitting at the foot of her mother's bed: sobbed uncontrollably, stopping her mouth with wet fingers and wet locks of hair, her eyes shut, hiding from the light.

'That's terrible, Lidochka — but one can understand his point of view as well, you know,' her mother said hesitantly. 'After all, he has two sets of commitments... It's a bit hard to demand clear-cut action from someone in that position. I'ts only the most primitive types who find taking decisions easy, whereas...'

'Yes, Mummy, yes, you're right! But you asked me a question, and I gave you my answer, and that's all there is to it. God forbid that I should ever interfere in his domestic life! What he's done for me already is quite enough. No, I have to sort everything out for myself — everything! Only what am I to do with Koko — leave him again?'

'Come and lie down, Lidochka, you're shaking all over! My poor dear girl, come and lie down!'

She buried her wet, burning face against her mother's shoulder, pulling over it the bedcover, her hair and a corner of the pillow, and wept, choking and murmuring something in a hoarse whisper, as if she had found at long last in this maternal shoulder and maternal warmth something to cling to; while her mother stroked her hair, her perspiring forehead, her wet hands, and said nothing.

The first autumn of the war was wet and cold. There was something doomed about the businesslike determination with which people had thrown themselves into their changed circumstances; it was as if they had all suddenly remembered the rules by which one should live, having somehow managed to forget them before. White phantom visions of old words and phrases hung in the air, demanding to be learned anew: medical supplies, military transports, mobilization, deserter, offensive. Hospitals were already full to overflowing. Along railway lines carrying sturdy bow-legged muzhiks in uniform off to the front, women's tears and ritualized peasant lamentation were the order of the day, with washed-out kerchiefs torn from windswept heads and held out in frozen valediction after departing trains. It was rumoured that the French course would be closed down any day, although on the surface at least the chaotically colourful life of Moscow went on as before.

Sasha was found unfit for military service and, feeling at a loose end, decided for the time being to stay with his parents in

Tambov. First, however, he stopped off in Moscow to see his sisters, accompanied by Alexander, who had enrolled at the Tver Artillery Academy.

Their train was badly delayed, and she was frozen in the thin high-heeled shoes she had slipped on, quite regardless of the weather, merely because she wanted to make an immediate impression. They jumped down from the high step of the carriage and ran towards her, waving their caps. Sasha looked thinner and paler than before, while Alexander (and this she noticed at once) was quite delighted to see her, his whole face lighting up. She gathered up the hem of her chequered skirt and glided towards them, wrinkling her nose against the smoke from the engine.

'Hello, Liza! Dear Liza,' said Sasha, coughing, as he embraced her. 'Have you been waiting long?'

'How you've changed!' exclaimed Alexander, clasping the cold hand she offered in both of his. 'You look more grown-up now!'

And more beautiful? asked her radiant eyes.


Because of the war Nikolay Vasilyevich was on hospital duty three nights a week now, returning home towards morning. Lydia was usually asleep. He would stamp noisily past her room with his shoes on and spend a long time making more noise in the dining room drinking tea and rustling his newspaper. Eventually he would roll up the newspaper and go through the corridor into the left-hand half of the house, where he would pull the nursery door ajar and make the sign of the cross over his sleeping son from the doorway, then, balancing on tiptoe, return to his study and lie down on the leather sofa, invariably in the same position: face-up, with his hands behind his head.

He had noticed a deterioration in his wife's health: in the mornings her feet were swollen, and by evening a feverish flush would appear on her face. However, he went through the motions of persuading himself that anything that happened to Lydia concerned him only in so far as it affected their child.

Returning from hospital duty one Thursday night, Nikolay Vasilyevich saw a light burning in the dining room and, seated round the table, his wife, her younger sister Liza, her brother Sasha, and a fourth person he did not know: a broad-shouldered man of medium height with a handsome face of a clear dark complexion.

Lydia was sitting on the sofa with her legs tucked under her, as was her habit. Her face was brightly flushed and there was a feverish glint in her eyes as she sat, her plait of curly light-brown hair draped over one shoulder, listening to Sasha. Greeting everyone and introducing himself to the stranger, Nikolay Vasilyevich joined them at the table and with a feeling of irritation poured himself some tea.

'I take a Tolstoyan view of war,' Sasha was saying, coughing gently and dabbing at his lips with a handkerchief. 'Whatever you may say, war is always murder — senseless murder, contrary to human nature. I'd be more prepared to defend duelling, if you like, because duels do have a certain logic to them as a rule. Two people meet and sort out their differences. It may be harsh, but that's how the world is, and living in this world as we do, we're constantly sorting out our differences with each other. We do it in all sorts of ways, sometimes with a weapon in our hands. But that's a personal, individual and in my view human sorting-out of differences, whereas war removes the element of personal conflict between people — removes it completely. People are reduced to mere objects, depersonalized. That's why I'm glad that the state of my health allows me the option of not participating in it.'

'And I'm glad that the state of my health does allow me to participate!' announced Alexander with a hearty laugh. 'In peacetime we still harbour illusions that everything is relatively well-ordered, that everything is going well, and if we do suffer some misfortune, we perceive it as our own individual, subjective misfortune and feel outraged at the injustice we've been subjected to. War is a communal affair, so in a war it should become apparent whether or not there's some hidden meaning to an existence in which everybody suffers. Or to put it more plainly, whether there is in this life a Godhead independent of all external circumstance. So for me it's a case of make or break — I'm going to war to sort out my differences with heaven, to test my suppositions...'

'Good Lord, what children you are!' frowned Nikolay Vasilyevich. 'Going to war to sort out your differences with the world? Romanticism of the first water! War is least of all a stage, and even less a laboratory in which experiments are carried out. War is war — an unavoidable evil which we had no hand in creating. And in a war people don't philosophize, they try to survive. You won't find any God or lofty meaning of life when you're sitting in a trench or bivouacking in snow in some forest. It's all much simpler, on the one hand, and...'

'I don't agree with you there,' Lydia suddenly interrupted him, flushing, and tossing her plait over her shoulder. 'I don't agree, because if someone has to suffer when everything around him is more or less going well, he becomes terribly self-centred and retreats into himself, and then he's finished, done for as a person. But a war reveals terrible suffering to us, human suffering as such, don't you agree? And war reminds us of God in the sense that we begin to think more about others and less about ourselves. Yes, war does demand our participation — not in the savagery, not in the destruction, but on the contrary, above all in acts of mercy, of charity...'

'Well, well, well...' said Nikolay Vasilyevich with a forced laugh, clicking the sugar tongs together. 'That sounds to me like the Smolny Institute talking! And how specifically do you envisage such participation?'

'I? Quite simply — I shall go on a nursing course, and when I've qualified I'll do voluntary service in a military hospital. A lot of women do it, there's nothing remarkable about it.'

'I'm lost for words,' said Nikolay Vasilyevich, throwing up his hands in despair. 'What about your health, have you thought about that?'

Sensing that the conversation was drifting into delicate matrimonial waters, Alexander stood up. 'We must have worn you out with all our philosophizing,' he said. 'It's time we were going.'

'But where will you possibly go now, in the middle of the night?' Lydia blushed in some confusion. 'Please, why don't you stay here. Sasha can sleep in the dining room, you in Nikolay Vasilyevich's study, and Liza with me or in the small parlour...'

'Liza will be better off in the small parlour,' Nikolay Vasilyevich interjected firmly. 'Otherwise Koko'll come running in at the crack of dawn and she won't get a proper night's sleep.'

Was that yellow Arbat house of mine, strewn with wet leaves of the first autumn of war, asleep, or pretending to sleep? Was

Alexander asleep in the study with its leather upholstery and stale odours of tobacco; was Sasha asleep, having managed to overcome his coughing? I don't know, I don't know.

I wasn't asleep when Nikolay Vasilyevich came into the bedroom in his grey dressing-gown and cautiously lay down on his half of the wide bed we had once shared.

'Are you asleep, Lydia?' he asked quietly.

'No. What do you want?'

'Were you serious about that course?'

'Absolutely. Why are you so surprised?'

She pulled the bedcover up to her chin and looked straight ahead. Waves of warmth came from the large-framed body lying motionless next to her. His weary eyes gazed brightly at her. She suddenly wanted to lay her head on his shoulder.

'I'm surprised because I realize how extremely foolhardy such a step would be. You're not in the best of health, and over-exertion of that kind could finish you off...' He broke off and corrected himself: 'I mean, could ruin your health irreparably.'

His voice was calm. With the palm of his large hand, which smelled of iodine, he gently turned my face towards him.

'Lydia, my dear, look at me.'

I looked at him. Here I was, lying next to my husband, the father of my child, aware of the forgotten, familiar warmth of his body. How tired I was!

'You're tired, Lydia, my dear. You're suffering from nervous exhaustion. I can't pretend to you any more — I'm terribly concerned about all this. Let me examine your feet: I just happened to notice this morning how swollen they were. And I'm not very happy about your pale complexion, or the way you get out of breath going up stairs. You need to think about dealing seriously with all this, instead of insisting on chasing after those ideas of out-dated patriotism and, as you say, charity...'

He threw back the bedcover and felt my feet with his warm hands. I did not move. He looked up at me with shining, careworn eyes. I covered my face with my hands, which were wet in an instant.

'Don't cry, please don't cry,' he said quietly. 'Don't cry, my darling. No-one is to blame for anything.'

And then — without reflecting, without wondering if I might do so — I drew towards him impulsively and laid my head on his shoulder.


The rainy season was over, and now the whole of Moscow looked bright and sparkling-clean from freshly fallen snow. How quickly she had grown accustomed to this city, to the flat the three of them shared, to cold tea with a white roll in the mornings, to the absence of servants, and to the loneliness.

The loneliness had come at once, as soon as she had sensed that she was no longer a child. What still remained of childhood was being eradicated by tortured dreams at night and a quite inexplicable anxiety by day. She would wake up with a headache, and so irritable that she felt like crying. Musya had become distant all of a sudden, and she didn't feel like going to Lydia's. In Lydia's face and in the movements of her spare, well-proportioned body she sometimes picked up echoes of her own dark dreams. It was particularly disturbing to come across her sitting as still as a statue on the sofa with her legs tucked under her, twisting her dishevelled plait of curly hair round her forefinger, her face registering complete detachment, almost blindness, yet at the same time kindled from within, lit by a happiness which surged in brief electric waves through her half-closed eyes, her half-open lips, her arching neck. Lydia was living in her own unknowable world, a world which no torments or terrors, not even her approaching illness, could bring her to renounce.

In any case their meetings had become infrequent now, as Lydia had got her own way and was working in a military hospital, from where she would return home late, half dead with fatigue. Nikolay Vasilyevich (as Liza noted with surprise) had become somehow strangely affectionate towards his wife.

Alexander hadn't shown up at all, and her desire to see him had become an obsession. She found it hard to visualize how it would be. Should she declare her love for him? But how? She could simply say: 'Alexander, I can't live without you,' and then go up to him and put her hands on his shoulders. And then he would embrace her. No, that was no good. She shut her eyes to see it all in detail. There he was coming in, covered in snow: serious, with dark shining eyes, looking at her but not smiling. Now he was holding out his rather small, yet broad hand. And then, while her hand was in his, she would say: 'I can't live without you. Marry me!' God, how stupid! Absolutely pathetic, declaring one's love to a man first. But where in heaven's name was he? When would she see him?

She saw him before he left for the front. Already the snow was thawing. The streets were awash with clamouring muddied streams, into which from high above the sun plunged its fevered head, rejoicing beyond measure at the sound of water, the smell of earth, the sight of windows flung open to the air.

They walked along Nikitsky Boulevard. Her agitation made her pace irregular, and she kept veering towards him so that her shoulder brushed his, making her falter in her step. Perhaps it really would be better to take a deep breath and say, 'Marry me!' rather than go on agonizing like this? A blind man with a black bandage over his eyes walked past, grey-haired and down at heel, carrying a stick which he tapped against the trees. He wore the Cross of St George in the buttonhole of his faded tunic...

Alexander watched him go. 'That's what I'm afraid of,' he said. 'Not death — although the thought of that's horrible enough too, and do you know why? Not because I might go to hell, or because this spring and our meeting would be finished then. No, I'm afraid of the unknown. I don't know what death will bring: Perhaps a void, a cessation of being; or perhaps something that no-one alive can even imagine. The fact is, all our guesses as to what will happen then are motivated purely by fear. Although... I don't know, perhaps there are certain cold intellects for whom the mystery of our existence or (who knows?) non-existence beyond the grave evokes mere curiosity. As for me, I can't even imagine curiosity of that abstract sort. Just fear, sheer undiluted fear at the thought that death is going to happen come what may, and that none of us can avoid it, could drive one to devote one's whole life to this mystery and not take notice of anything else...'

'But you just said you weren't afraid of death,' she remarked, seeing only the dark complexion of his face, his shining eyes, and the delicate bridge of his nose, above which his wide eyebrows were knitted in a tangle of wispy down.

'Did I really say that?' he smiled.

Hungrily her open lips took in the velvet tones, so dear to her, of his voice.

'Did I really say that?' he repeated, serious now. 'You misunderstood me. I am afraid of death, but even more of physical disfigurement, especially blindness. You know, I even go to sleep with the light on. They used to come down really heavily on me for that when I was a child to try and break me of the habit: I'd have to stand in the corner and go without pudding. No, I couldn't do without light to save my life.'

'Yes,' she whispered. 'Yes, of course. But I still can't believe it's true that you're going to the front, and so soon, and that you could be...'

She sank down on a bench, pressing to her lips a wet glove she had removed from her hand. He bent over and suddenly took her face, which was raised towards him, between both hands. He held her face between the palms of his hands, and the two of them froze in a posture which must have looked odd to any passer-by: she, holding a wet glove crammed against her mouth, perched on the edge of a wet bench to which still clung remnants of black frozen-on snow; and he squeezing her cheeks between the palms of his hands as firmly as if, instead of holding a woman's face, he were clasping the trunk of a tree to keep his balance.

'What is it?' he whispered at last. 'What?'

And then, gazing steadily into his shining eyes, her own eyes transfixed with fear, she said, 'I can't live without you. Marry me!'

That evening they sat without lighting the lamp on opposite sides of the table, which was spread with a white cloth. It was as if there were only two colours, black and white, left in the whole world; for outside the window heavy snow had started tumbling from the sky without warning, absorbing all other sounds into the even, muffled sound of its falling, its whiteness contrasting with dark objects in the dusk-enveloped room: the table at which they were sitting; the wooden frame of the bed beneath its counterpane of a whiteness seeming to match that outside; the silvery mirror in its black frame like some cold, sequestered inlet of a lake; her thin wrist in the black sleeve of her jacket.

'Tell me,' he begged her. 'Tell me everything about yourself, don't be afraid. I was so afraid you'd turn out to be someone else — someone I'd just met by chance and didn't really know.'

'What have I turned out to be, then?' she asked with a nervous laugh which died away again immediately; and stretching her black-sleeved arms across the white tablecloth, she placed her hands in his open palms.

'What do you think?' he said, squeezing her hands.

'I keep worrying that I might start saying something to make you stop loving me, that you might think me stupid and uneducated.'

'Uneducated? Don't be silly, what does that matter? God knows, you couldn't exactly call me educated...'

'No, but Sasha said...'

'Sasha's an ass. He thinks if you read three Greek tragedies you'll be three times more intelligent as a consequence. Whereas, the way I see it, the most important thing is simply life itself. Go out into the world and know it — isn't that right?'

'Yes. Lord, how happy I am! How I understand everything you say! How calm I am when I'm with you! With you I feel so...'

He carefully pulled her hands towards him, and obediently she followed after, drawn towards him across the table, closer and closer to his face, which gleamed faintly white in the darkness, and to his open lips, searching in the darkness for hers.

'I'll come back from the front, and then we'll get married. You know, I had our future life together mapped out a long time ago. I'll show you my poems — they were all written for you, every single one. I wanted you to be there, to appear. I wanted to prove myself worthy of you. Do you understand?'

'Yes, yes. Wait, I'll come and sit next to you. You're pulling me across the table — we're going to knock it over...'

Without letting go of his hands, she moved to another chair. Now she sat with her hands resting on his shoulders, and their two faces were separated by a frail, quivering tissue of ethereal winter darkness.

'How I shall miss you and pray for you — every hour, every minute of the day!'

'I'll get some leave if I can manage to distinguish myself in some way. They award it like that, as an incentive.'

'Distinguish yourself? Does that mean you'll be wounded?'

'Not necessarily. But I'll get back to you, some way or another.'

'Just promise me, Alexander: if you are wounded... My God, I don't even want to talk about it! But whatever happens, however badly wounded you might be, don't have any doubts about me, come back to me — that's more important than anything else!'

Now it is snowing so heavily I can hardly hear a thing. What was that he just whispered? I love you? No, I think it was something else. But now she is speaking:

'Lala and Musya have gone away. Musya's at her aunt's, and Lala's in Tambov. She's had terrible news — her brother's been killed. Seryozha, her elder brother.'

Why doesn't he reply? Or is it that I can't hear him? And why is it suddenly snowing like this? It's well into spring, after all.

'You are my wife now — fiancée, wife, it makes no difference. But nothing will happen between us — you do understand me, don't you? Until I return from the front and we're joined in the sight of God, I have no right to that.'

Their faces, gleaming faintly white, were no longer separated by ethereal winter darkness. She had rested her forehead on his chin.

'I'm not afraid of anything.'

'But I'm afraid for you. You're still a child, I know, although to me you're the most adorable woman there could be. I just want to look at you and then leave at once — may I do that? I'll leave at once, I promise...'

His fingers trembled as he unbuttoned her black jacket. She sat in front of him, holding her breath, this girl of dark complexion in the linen chemise sewn for her by the family dressmaker, with thin shoulder-straps and a narrow band of cream-coloured lace at the chest. How she had pleaded before leaving for Moscow: 'Couldn't it have just a bit more lace, Mummy?' 'You're going there to study!' her mother had snapped. 'What do you want with lace?'

She sat in front of him, holding her breath.

'I just want to look at you, then I'll leave at once. And I shall remember this for the rest of my life...'

Bending to feel with open lips the fearful beating of her heart, her dark-skinned warmth beneath the thick linen, he whispered, 'I shall always be with you, always...'

\* \* \*

'Why do I think there's no life after death?'

She is half-reclining on the low creaking couch on our dacha veranda, swinging her foot in its well-worn slipper and flicking ash into the lid of a pickle jar. The oil stove is humming, and the birch tree in front of the steps scatters dappled leaf-shadows across the veranda. There's something else, too... A fragrant smell of some sort... Of course, it's raspberry jam, still runny and covered with muslin to keep the flies off, cooling down at the top of the steps.

'Why do I think there's no life after death? Because if there were, he'd have found some way to get in touch with me in all this time — forty years, it's been! At the very least he'd have come to me in a dream, or I'd have caught a glimpse of him somewhere. I couldn't imagine a more sensitive soul. That's why I think if *he*'s disappeared without trace, there must be nothing at all after we die...'

'With fingers light as airy dreams...' muttered Nikolay Vasilyevich, dropping three lumps of sugar into his tea. 'Why are you looking so despondent, Liza?'

'I've come to see Lydia. Is she asleep?'

'She may well be. Give her a knock. Don't you want any tea?'

'No thanks. I'll give her a knock then, all right?'

She was sleeping with a grey shawl draped over her. Her face was careworn, her eyelids dark with fatigue. Her hair — auburn and heavy where plaited, curly and golden on her temples and neck — covered her right cheek, and she lay with her left cheek resting on her cupped hands, as she had done as a child. She always slept like that. Even when she died, in her sleep, it was in that same position. But now she was just asleep, her thin hand on the grey shawl gently backlit by the setting sun of the nascent spring outside. Koko and his nanny were cracking nuts and whispering in the nursery.

She opened her eyes.

'Have you been to see him off?'

'I've just got back. Talk to me. I shall die without him.'

'Good heavens, what makes you think you'll take any note of what I have to say? You feel now that your whole life is centred on him and nobody else, don't you? But if I were to tell you that your life is just beginning, and that he's just a first entanglement, a trial run, what then? You wouldn't believe me, would you, you'd take offence.'

'How dare you talk to me like that, how dare you! I come to you as my sister, my only friend, and all you can do is fling sordid platitudes of that sort in my face! I'm going again, this instant!'

'Liza, my pet, what's the matter? Why be so upset? I wish you happiness from the bottom of my heart, only I think that...'

'You think! Of course, when it's you, then it's something quite out of this world, then it's perfectly all right to abandon your child and moon around in Paris for God knows how long, and then be forgiven for everything — isn't that so? But he's gone off to the front, any day he could be... And you talk to me of an *entanglement!*'

She sobbed this last word into Lydia's grey shawl with its smell of mothballs, held tightly in her sister's arms and with her wet face pressed to her chest.

'Lizochka, please forgive me, I don't know what I'm saying. There's so much heartache inside me that I end up letting it out on others. It's all because I feel so lonely and bitter. Don't you think I know how much I've changed? But what can I do? You know, it's a terrible thing to say, but I even volunteered for hospital work just as a way of escaping from myself. There are these dressings I have to do, which are awful, because the wounds have gone gangrenous and you daren't even breathe in near them, let alone look at them. Men die in my arms, and I close their eyes with these hands! Do you remember that little baby bird we found when we were at the dacha once? You must have been about seven and I was thirteen, and we'd gone with Antonina Pavlovna in that funny wagonette to pick berries, do you remember? I picked the little thing up and wrapped it in my handkerchief, but it started fluttering its wings and cheeping its poor little heart out as soon as the wagonette moved off. Then it started foaming at the mouth, and just before we got home it died in my hands. Do you remember how I cried? I was so devastated — it had been so alive, so warm, cheeping away, and then suddenly it was nothing more than a little bundle in my hands, a stiff little bundle. That stayed with me for years afterwards. But now it's people dying in my arms, one after the other, and I actually go into that smoking inferno of pain of my own accord — not because I'm some kind of saint, but because I simply can't stand my own company!'

'Lydia, what is it that's troubling you so much? Why not get it off your chest?'

'My dear, you say, "Get it off your chest" like that... You've never even seen him, have you? Even if you had, you wouldn't understand. The truth of it is that I'm completely and utterly attached to him, bound to him irrevocably. He's no angel, you can believe me, but I accept him with all his shortcomings, and nothing he did would ever surprise me. Oh, if only you knew how changeable he can be! Sometimes he can be off-hand, matter-of-fact, ironic, almost a stranger; yet at other times he's just a little boy, like Koko... God, I can't bear to talk about him! It's like changing a dressing on myself, having to tear it away where it's dried on to the wound... And what about Nikolay Vasilyevich, what's he done to deserve all this? How many times I've tried to go back to my old life, tried to find some sort of peace and draw a line under these last three years!

How many times we've broken it off! Do you know, even in Paris I tried to leave him. Suddenly I decided I couldn't go on like this any more, that I had to go back to Moscow. I kept having dreams about Koko every night — I had this awful feeling there was something wrong with him that people were hiding from me in their letters. Apart from which we'd been quarrelling and bickering... Even so I didn't feel I could go straight back to Moscow and break with him completely, so I got on a train early one morning and headed south, leaving an off-hand little note that said nothing really. I stayed in this little boarding house, and it was all so terribly depressing. I was terrified that it might all be finished between us now, that all I'd succeeded in doing by going there was to make him feel resentful. After all, men don't like that sort of drama at all — they have this acute embarrassment about expressing feelings, this fear of absolute transparency in relationships, do you know what I mean? But to get back to the point... It was really warm there, the birds were singing, and there I was — sick at heart, unable to eat, just sitting on my own in that godforsaken little room, and thinking. And then on the evening of the third day the door suddenly opened and he came in... I threw myself into his arms like a mad thing...'

Suddenly she blushed deeply and hid her face in her hands.

'What's the matter, Lidochka?' Liza whispered.

'What's the matter? We can only find some kind of peace when we're together — physically together, do you understand? My God, what am I saying!'

'Never mind, Lydia, I understand, I understand! Only... What is it that's really troubling you?'

Lydia took hold of her auburn plait with its fine-spun threads of gold and pressed it to her eyes.

'Everything. I came across something in a book once about love being stronger, the more fragile it is. That's strange, isn't it, yet it does seem to be true. I think our love is pure fragility. Do you think I feel jealous on his account? Well, I don't. I don't trust him, and that's worse than anything.'

'Does he deceive you, then?'

'Not deliberately. He doesn't so much deceive me anyway, as — how shall I put it? — betrays me — although he doesn't really mean to and, what's worse, doesn't even know he's doing it. He betrays me by being too concerned for his own well-being, unwilling to take risks on my account. Without realizing it, he's cast me in a particular role in his life, and a deeply humiliating one at that.'

Liza had drawn closer and was now stroking her chin with the end of her sister's dishevelled plait. The glowing sunset swathed their arms and shoulders ever more tightly in its dry gold and kindled the fine partings in their curly hair, before finally disappearing.

'What role is that, Lydia?'

Lydia's unseeing eyes skimmed across her sister's puckered brow.

'The leading role: his mistress. It's quite simple really. If you think of his life — with his wife, his children, his job — in terms of a letter, then I'm the P.S. You know the sort of thing people write: "Oh, I nearly forgot..." Never: "I forgot the most important thing," but always that: "I nearly forgot..." P.S., in short. But let's close the subject now, Liza, I couldn't tell you the half of it even if I tried. Let's go and find Koko, I haven't really seen him to speak of today.'

She shrugged off the fluffy shawl and stood up, holding both hands to her hair. The sunlight swept across her face and faded from her parting.

'Lydia, one last thing: will Alexander come back to me? What does your heart tell you?'

Each gazed into the other's tearful eyes that were so like her own.

'Why do you even ask, Liza, of course he'll come back!'

He was buried by flying earth from a shell crater during the Brusilov offensive, when the Russian army went over to the attack. Thank God, he suffered none of the things he had feared so much. His leg was not torn off, nor was his tongue crushed; and the darkness which fell upon him had nothing in it of divine retribution for his weakness of will and childish fears, for it was not blindness, but simply death...

\* \* \*

Wait now, my delicate-winged one, my joy: surely you must be tired of circling back and forth above me? What dark foreboding troubles you? Are you afraid I might get carried away and start making things up? Do you think I might suddenly dissolve in tears and blurt out: 'Oh, no! That broad-shouldered man with the dark complexion and dark eyes who was swallowed up by the earth — that wasn't him at all, it wasn't Alexander, but...' Don't worry yourself on that score, let's forget about that...

It's something else that concerns me now. Many, many things were sucked into that crater: the dark room with its untouched white bed, witness of their impassioned conversation; the promise of a life lived in loving harmony; those poems written in purple copybooks...

But was that really all? Spinning as she fell, scattering buttons from her cream-coloured chemise, she too was sucked into it, that girl with lips like the sun-warmed water lilies they had once picked together on the lake, leaning over the side of that leaky rowing boat; and with her went all her family, together with all the ordinary trials and tribulations offered by a life not yet reduced to the level of mere survival, not yet deprived of its profoundly human lineaments: a nephew on a white rocking-horse, lemon-coloured lamplight in the house of one's parents, naive plans for the future...

As for me, sitting here poised with pencil in hand on the Boston grass, that death in the all-engulfing earth also leaves me with no option but to recast my whole narrative, having failed in my attempts to dress it up as the chronicling of family tradition and to fit it around those letters I pored over during hot July days of my adolescence spent lying in the sweet-scented shade of an apple tree, stretched out in the long grass with its scatterings of richly gleaming buttercups, savouring that smell, so dear to me, of raspberry jam stood to cool on the veranda steps...

\* \* \*

'Why do you say shoppin'? Why can't you pronounce words properly? And do you have to dress like some scruffy old tramp? Look at Lala — she's never let herself go like that!'

I am at that awkward transitional age when I find everything about life annoying, and especially my grandmother. In her quest to become more like common people which she began in 1917 she really went overboard. Standing in queues, where her outward appearance allows her to blend in effortlessly, she has acquired habits of sloppy pronunciation and down-to-earth in speaking, not to mention a penchant for unwashed handkerchiefs. Yet she mutters French in her sleep! And those awful cheap-and-nasty Belomor cigarettes of hers! We have friends of mine coming to the flat whose fathers travel to East Germany and Bulgaria on official business, and there'll be my grandmother puffing away like a lorry driver, stubbing out her squat fag-ends in the lid of a pickle jar. My dented pride is temporarily restored when we suddenly acquire a stylish sideboard of East German make with four blue chairs, so that now our rooms in Plyushchikha Street begin to bear at least some distant resemblance to the apartments of those daughters of the Party élite whose friendship I seek and whose shoes I dream of at nights.

'You're bourgeois, that's what you are,' she says sadly. 'I can't think where you get it from.'

'I don't care if I am bourgeois, Grandma — just don't say shoppin', and stop smoking!'

It was to be many years before I came to appreciate her Belomor cigarettes, her skilful rendition of mispronunciations heard in queues, the Chopin waltzes she played in the evenings on our out-of-tune piano with its cracked lid...

\* \* \*

'Nurse! For charity's sake, love, let me take some poison or summat. Look at what's left o' me — naught but a stump, a useless block o' wood fit to chuck on't fire! I shall finish meself off anyway, even if I have no hands to do it. Please help me on me way, love, there's a good lass!'

Stars were falling from the sky. She stood on the front steps of the hospital, her fingers locked round the handrail, her head spinning. She wouldn't faint, was determined not to. The hospital forecourt swam before her eyes. The stars were falling with unnatural frequency, each making, it seemed to her, a slight thud on impact. There was another one. And another. Merciful God in heaven, she thought, how I want to die! To lie down on these steps and lay my head on my hands. 'Help me, nurse, for charity's sake!' But what about me, who'll show me any charity?

It's finished. Yesterday we finally parted. I always knew it would come to that. Don't you remember how even during the good times together I always knew it would come to that? That's what made me do all those crazy things — I seized each moment breathlessly, afraid of losing time. And now it's happened. Oh God, help me! How am I going to get through all this? He wanted to leave, and that's what he did. Where did he go? To his wife's parents in Saratov. Why Saratov? It's just the way things have turned out. The way what's turned out? I don't know, don't remember. He's been exempted from military duty. But what's Saratov got to do with it? He did say something... I just can't remember. All I remember are his hands. Not even his hands, just my body caressed by his hands. 'I'll be back again in three or four months, look after yourself.' Lies! It's all over, isn't it. Oh God, help me! How am I going to get through this? Look, another star — falling, falling... gone.

'You have to understand, Anya, I only ever saw him once. What can I tell you about him? She clammed up completely. I knew he had a family, and that he was an artist and quite well-to-do. She once laughingly compared herself to the heroine of Chekhov's story, "A Flighty Woman". Her husband was a doctor too, you see, and her lover an artist. But otherwise she kept the whole thing to herself. Took it to the grave with her, and bore the suffering all on her own...'

\* \* \*

I want to go home. Stars are falling, my head's spinning. Home. Where's my child? Oh, so now you've remembered your child. Do you really think I ever forgot him?

'Lydia, go to the door! Do you hear me, Lydia?'

His face trembling, Nikolay Vasilyevich was drawing an oily liquid into a syringe. Koko lay asleep, sprawled on the double bed in his parents' room, his face flushed bright red. Snatches of wheezing breath broke unevenly from his little chest.

Have I been asleep? she thought.

Her tousled auburn head was resting on the bedcover, through which were outlined the contours of a child's knees. She'd simply gone out like a light there at his feet after two nights without sleep. Nikolay Vasilyevich was sure it wasn't diphtheria. She just prayed to God he was right. He'd been walking up and down all night with Koko in his arms, and she'd followed him around like a shadow. How she revered those large, plump hands drawing the oily liquid into the syringe! Their whole life together had been a mistake, and she alone was to blame. If only Koko would pull through! He'd been coughing in his sleep, so hard sometimes that he'd ended up vomiting. It was only now, towards morning, that he'd become calmer. How could she have fallen asleep?

'Go to the door, Lydia!'

She forced herself up and staggered into the hall. There were three shadows standing outside the door: a large one in the middle, flanked by two smaller ones. The larger one, pallid and wrapped in a black head-scarf, fell at her feet.

'Oh missis, dear lady, please help us! Our house has burned down, we've no roof over our heads, and we're tryin' to get to my auntie in Tula. My husband's away fightin' in the war. Help us, for charity's sake!'

That word again: it was pursuing her. Herself a tousled auburn shadow, she bent over the black head-scarf, trying to pull

it away from her feet. Four shadows in the doorway of a house in
the Arbat, beneath the falling stars. She took a step backwards,
and the black head-scarf crawled after her, keening loudly.

'Come in, come in!'

'Oh, we couldn't possibly do that, we're all full of lice from
travellin'! Please just let us have whatever you can spare for the
children. I was just talkin' to the woman what sweeps your yard,
and she says: go and ask the doctor's wife, go and ask her now!'

'Lydia, see to Koko, I'll deal with this.'

Behind her loomed the figure of Nikolay Vasilyevich.
Steadying herself against the doorpost, she watched him stuff
bread, cooked meat, soap, a rug and money into their fleshless
hands, their pockets, their depleted haversacks, and heard the two
little muffled-up shadows already breathing noisily with delight
as they gnawed away at some lumps of sugar.

'You're a Christian, sir!' cried the large pallid figure in the
black headscarf. 'I shall never forget your kindness! I shall
remember you in my prayers!'

'Not me, not me,' he said hastily, glancing anxiously over his
shoulder. 'Don't pray for me, my dear, pray for God's servants
Nikolay and Lydia...'

\* \* \*

Koko died not long ago. He'd come back from Magadan,
where he'd spent his exile after release from the camps, and then
married a nurse from Botkin Hospital. He always wanted to buy
a headstone for his father's grave in Vagankov Cemetery, but there
was never enough money, and nothing ever came of it.

# Part Two

*T*hat tram clanking past behind me sounds for all the world like the Moscow trams of my childhood. How hot it is here in Boston this summer! You feel you just can't breathe. I must try and think about something else instead.

How old would I have been then... ten? That's right, ten. I'd been diagnosed by this top specialist as having suspected cancer of the kidneys — no laughing matter, even if he wasn't absolutely sure about it. I had to go into hospital for tests, which were supposed to last a week. My father sent me jokey little notes, promising me visits to Luzhniki sports stadium on Saturday and the Children's World department store on Sunday, and I just counted the minutes. The tests were painful.

'He drank every evening. Came home from work, rang the doctor in attendance, and then hit the bottle. Wouldn't eat a thing, said he couldn't. I tried to reassure him as best I could — I just had this feeling that there was nothing wrong with you. My God, he paid them so much they'd have been quite happy to say you'd got the plague! And that doddery old professor didn't even have all his faculties any more. I kept telling your father, "There's nothing wrong with her." But he would insist, "No, let's have her examined by another doctor." I don't know how we got through that week. I tell you, every evening he sat there, nursing a bottle.

He never got drunk, though. If the phone rang, he'd jump up and run to it as if he had a rocket under him.'

Of course, he wasn't drunk. He wasn't drunk, but he felt wretchedly weak, and his face was wet with tears. There was a knock at the door. Standing outside were a man and a girl of about nine. The man, lean and unshaven, wore a padded jacket scorched through on the chest. The girl kept her face buried in his sleeve.

'Could you help us, sir,' said the man. 'Our house has burned down.'

What a godsend, and how he seized on the man, urging him, 'Come in, sit down!'

And how too the woman with the dark complexion and lively dark eyes, then still in her prime, began to fuss over the sallow-faced little girl, having first stubbed out her cigarette in the lid of a pickle jar! Yet the girl shrank from her, shivering and hiding her face in the sleeve of her father's scorched jacket.

'Our house has burned down,' the man repeated, perching cautiously on the edge of the faded reddish-brown sofa. 'We lost everything we had in the fire, and now we're on our way to relatives. I've no wife any more — me and my daughter have to struggle along as best we can.'

He ransacked all the cupboards, his hands shaking. This overcoat, a jacket, a warm sweater for the girl (if only everything turns out all right, he thought, if only they don't find anything, I'll gladly buy another one for my little girl!), shoes, and warm underwear, and... His hands were shaking. Perhaps he was slightly drunk after all?

'What am I to do with all this, sir? It'd take half a dozen people just to carry it!'

'Take it, take it! If you don't need it, I'm sure your daughter will. Now we'll get you both something to eat, and I'll give you some money. Have you far to go?'

And then the unshaven man in the scorched jacket began to shake uncontrollably, at the same time clasping the shivering little girl to him and emitting a strange sound like the muffled baying of a dog.

They left the following morning.

'I shall never forget your kindness,' the man said in a hoarse voice, bowing to them. The girl bowed as well.

'Pray for us,' said the woman with the dark complexion and lively dark eyes. 'Pray for my granddaughter to come home, for her not to be ill.'

Two days later I was discharged from hospital. The tests had proved negative.

Lord, I know we are undeserving of Thy mercy, yet grant us Thy forgiveness. Give shelter to the soul on its journey through the ethereal regions, the soul that knows not where to turn, the soul that slipped out from that black headscarf. Give it shelter, Lord.


'Tulips, tulips, oh, my lovely tulips...'

The old woman shuffled across the ice-cold floor, her legs thin and varicose-veined. It was colder inside the room than out in the street. No heat at all came from the little stove, which had its flue pipe pushed through the ventilation opening at the top of the window. There was no firewood. She squatted down over a small chest with tinplate bindings, from which she proceeded to claw with thin fingers culminating in flattened brown nails some exercise books filled with small handwriting. It was the winter of 1919.

'Oh my tulips, poem-tulips, poems no-one reads... Oh my tulip-boy, my little joy, tulip's naughty deeds...'

She rocked with laughter, laughing so hard that tears came to her eyes. Her dark eyebrows knitted in a tangle of down above the bridge of her nose, and her eyes widened menacingly.

'And now,' she said, wagging her finger at no-one in particular, 'now they've killed my boy.' Again she rocked with laughter. 'And what's Mummy doing? Mummy's going to light the stove with these poems.' She shrugged her shoulders under her shabby fur stole. 'Alexander's going to keep Mummy warm. My boy wrote so many poems that Mummy'll be lovely and warm, ha-ha-ha!'

The door was not locked, and after the girl entered the freezing, junk-filled apartment it took a long time before the snow on her began to melt. She kept her gloveless hands, which were red and stiff with the cold, hidden inside her wet, shrivelled muff.

'His mother lives in Sadovo-Triumfalnaya Street. She wasn't all there even when Alexander was alive, so I shouldn't wonder if she's completely mad by now. I suppose you could drop by if you wanted to, you might find her there.'

Sasha was lying low in Tambov, expecting to be arrested again at any moment. She had left him and her parents in the basement of their expropriated house in what had once been Bolshaya Dvoryanskaya Street, where, together with her old nanny and her grandmother, they had been forced to move. Two floors of the house were now occupied by some Soviet government office.

Sasha hadn't wanted her to visit the crazed old woman. What would be the point? But she had noticed, not without some surprise, a peculiar hardening against loss and misfortune building up inside her. Sometimes it seemed as if it had always been like this: the damp rat-infested basement; the bucket of water encrusted with ice; her father lying wrapped in blankets, paralysed; her mother with hair as white as snow; her grandmother and nanny in identical padded jackets. Yes, it had always been like this, and it could only get worse. Now in response to her mother's pleas she had come to Moscow to be with Lydia. Even the appalling frustrations of the journey hadn't struck her as being anything out of the ordinary. It was as if she had known it all before in some distant former life.

As she entered the freezing, junk-filled apartment, she was not at all surprised to feel that she had seen this dark-eyed old woman with her moulting furs and offensive smell somewhere before. The old woman looked up from the chest, her eyes narrowing.

'Anyway,' she said without a flicker of surprise, 'let me ask you a question now: where are the matches?'

'My name's Liza.' Her own voice sounded strange. 'I was your son's fiancée.'

'Fiancée?' The old woman's black eyebrows knitted above the bridge of her nose. 'He didn't have a fiancée. Do you know what he had? He had his Mummy.'

'Very well,' she whispered. 'It's not important. Only he was very dear to me, and that's why I've come to see you.'

'You're not trying to imply that he's dead, I hope?' The old woman's head with its unkempt strands of grey hair was thrown back at a haughty angle. 'If so, you can forget it. Others have told me the same. He even assures me himself that he's been killed, but I just laugh at him. "Alexander", I say, "how can you have been killed if you're coming here to see me?" What nonsense! But then children do like those sorts of games, as I'm sure you must know.'

'What games?' She had begun to shiver, and not from the cold.

'Those dreadful games they play with the devil. Not the Evil One himself, you understand, it's the parents who play with him. No, children make friends with this little devil or demon who lures them away, who understands them. Well anyway, my son made friends with him too. He used to run away from me and hide in the raspberry bushes, and I knew he'd be meeting up with that little demon there. How many times I used to lie in wait for them! You know, I could just fancy a nice crusty roll.'

'A roll?' Her teeth were chattering.

'Yes, a roll,' said the old woman with a condescending smirk. 'I'm fed up with just herring heads all the time. And then I'd like some peaches, with a nice bloom on them. My husband always used to say my cheeks were like peaches, but I'd correct him and say: "No, it's the peaches that are like my cheeks." Ha-ha-ha! But what were we talking about? Ah yes, Alexander's games. That little demon started teaching him to write poetry, but poor Alexander was no good at it. He'd get frustrated and burn his poems in the stove. And then I saw...'

A yellow hand with dark knotted veins and arthritic joints

suddenly flew out from beneath the moulting furs and snapped its fingers in the air before disappearing again.

'And then I saw that little black demon, dressed in a black frock coat, go across to the stove and pull a sheet of paper out of the flames. He smoothed it out and said something to Alexander, who came alive and beamed all over his face. And do you know why that little black demon wanted my boy to write poetry?'

'No, why?' she asked, her lips white and trembling.

The old woman's hand with its flattened fingernails described a large circle in the air.

'Because poetry distracted Alexander from all this, from life. But in life you have to be on your guard. Already the orchards were being chopped down, but that little demon came and offered all the children something different: perhaps poetry, or a girl, or some idea that had a spell on it, do you see? Mmm, I'd really love a nice crusty roll!'

'What do you eat?' Liza asked, kneeling down in front of the chest with the tinplate bindings. 'What have you eaten today?'

'What do you think I've got him for?' the old woman retorted, narrowing her eyes haughtily. 'He'll bring me something, he always does. I'm not joking, he's my husband. We split up a long time ago, but he still loves me the same as before. Do you see in that saucepan there, the leg of mutton?'

She stood up from the floor and pulled a saucepan from under some rags. It contained a gnawed bone swimming in some remnants of grey soup.

'He got this in exchange for a cambric chemise, no expense spared,' she said triumphantly. 'And he'll bring me some more. Treats me like a queen, he does — he'll go without food himself, but always bring me some. He'd bake me some bread if I told him to, but I won't — I'd rather wait for Alexander to bring some. It's so nice to get bread from up there... What's up, would you like something to eat? Why are you staring at the saucepan like that?'

'No, no,' she whispered, 'I don't want anything. Please carry on...'

'Anyway, they'd already started chopping down the orchards here, but the boys wrote their poems or brooded over their own thoughts, as the little demon had taught them. They didn't notice that the orchards were being chopped down and needed saving, they missed all that. Alexander too, he was one of them. When he comes back, I'll ask him, "Why did you run away from me and hide in the raspberry bushes?" '

'What's in those copybooks?' asked Liza, finally managing to regain her composure. Next to the saucepan lay a pile of purple copybooks.

'Aha, so you've noticed them! It doesn't matter how well the little demon hides them, a loving woman will always find them, I know that. We'll burn them together now and warm ourselves up, then you won't need that dreadful muff — how can you carry a thing like that around? You'll be lovely and warm. When Alexander comes here again, I'll tell him, "You're free, they're gone." '

'We can't do that, those are his poems! Give them to me, please! I'll bring you firewood. Please don't burn them, I beg of you!'

'Are you serious? If I give them to you, Alexander will never come back. Ah, here are the matches — lovely matches, all my lovely tulips...'

Liza snatched up the small chest, which turned out to be quite heavy, and stuffed the copybooks into it. The old woman clawed at her with her flattened fingernails.

'Tell me, was it He who sent you?'

'Nobody sent me. Let me go!'

'My dear boy,' murmured the old woman, 'is that really what you want me to do — give them away?'

She rose from the floor and with a regal gesture flicked invisible dust from her skirt.

'Take them. I'm going to have a bit of that nice soup now. Yes, I'll have some soup, seeing as there are no rolls.'

'Did you see her again after that?'

'I went to see her throughout the three months I was with Lydia in Moscow. Nikolay Vasilyevich and I sawed up the walnut sofa and took firewood to her on a sledge. How could I abandon her? But after Lydia died I left Moscow straight away and never saw her again.'

'And the poems?'

'I treasured them for a long time. Later, when we were evacuated, we lost everything, the poems too.'

The house in the Arbat had been filled with new tenants. Nikolay Vasilyevich and his family were left with just two small rooms at the side of the house.

Nikolay Vasilyevich knelt in front of the little portable stove, trying to light the damp firewood inside. It gave off smoke, refusing to kindle properly, and he had repeatedly to rub his watering eyes with the back of his hand before again returning to the task in hand. The sound of subdued coughing could be heard through the partition wall. At last the firewood crackled into flame, and, rising heavily from his knees, he pushed the door to the adjoining room. She was lying on her side in her customary position with her pinched, careworn cheek resting on cupped hands. Every now and then she coughed in her sleep. Nikolay Vasilyevich straightened the bedcover, which had slipped off, and with an anxious frown felt her forehead. It was hot and dry.

'Lydia, my darling,' he said cautiously, 'it's time for your mustard poultices...'

She opened her eyes and gave him a startled, glazed look.

'You remember that boy who hid with us back in the summer?' she said. 'The one you took under your wing at the time? He told us about a case of cannibalism out in the country, and you didn't believe him at first, you said it was biologically impossible, do you remember?'

Nikolay Vasilyevich put his large hand on hers.

'Don't think about it, you mustn't over-excite yourself. Why do you have to go out of your way to torment yourself like that?'

'I remembered it as I was dropping off to sleep, and I could picture it all so vividly. You know, we used to read books, we brought our children up to be good, we shrank at the sound of strong language. Yet it was all a kind of children's game, a kind of self-delusion people were engaged in. All the time beneath that life which seemed on the face of it so attractive, so sanitised, with its music and starched table napkins, something else altogether was lurking: something bestial, bloody and brutal. Some village miles from anywhere in winter, with one person eating another — and no table napkins in sight... And while I was thinking about this, I fell asleep and dreamt that years ago I'd committed some crime myself, perhaps even eaten someone.'

'Me,' laughed Nikolay Vasilyevich.

'Wait, don't interrupt. I dreamt I'd done something terrible, but couldn't remember what it was or when I'd done it. In the dream I was trying to remember, but couldn't. It was as though it had happened in another life, and my soul could remember it but not put it into words. Actually, I was almost awake when you came in: just lying there, trying to remember. It was only when you bent over me that I really came to again and made myself wake up properly. Are you frightened?'

'No,' he said emphatically. 'You're letting yourself go, Lydia. Typhus patients have worse hallucinations than that, but they don't scare anyone. They're just ill, and that's all there is to it. But you nurse your emotions, you analyze them. These are harsh and frightening times, no-one would deny that. We've fallen under the wheels of an unstoppable train, all of us — but what does that mean? It means our hour has come, the time for us to be put to the test. As a doctor I've spent my whole life dealing with people who've fallen under the wheels of trains, figuratively speaking. I've got into the habit of searching for remedies, of fighting for life. Call me naive, but it seems to me that even this nightmare we're living through now will one day be a memory for those who survive, and a fact of history for those who don't — that all in all, one way or another, everything will come right again in the end, as it always has before.'

'Just a minute... Are you really not afraid?'

'Do you want to know the truth? I'm afraid for you and Koko, the two people who are dearer to me than anything else in the world. And I pray to God to spare you both — and me as well, because without me you won't be able to survive.'

'I feel hot,' she whispered, throwing off the quilt. 'I'm burning all over, yet before I was asleep I couldn't get warm at all. I've got a fever again, haven't I?'

'Probably,' he muttered evasively. 'I'll get you your medicine now, and some poultices.'

'Nikolay!' she cried, stretching out her almost transparent arms towards him. 'I'm so grateful, and I do love you so! I certainly don't deserve all this.'

'Lydia, my dear, what idiot told you that one can ever deserve love? Love is a strange business — always against the grain, always in spite of something, never because of it. And that's all as it should be, I assure you, Madame.'

He went out, and she lay back on the pillow again.

'My God!' she thought. 'I haven't seen you for nearly four years now, haven't had a letter for nearly two. Are you still alive? Are you alive, my beloved in spite of everything, my only beloved?

'Such a black sky out there, outside the iced-up window. I expect I shall be going soon. What's up there, in that black sky? Perhaps I shall never actually find out — perhaps I shall stay down in the frozen earth, with patched felt boots shuffling about above me, kicking the snow this way and that.'

Nikolay Vasilyevich appeared in the doorway, carrying a small basin from which rose a thin wisp of steam.

There was something I wanted to... Suffering, that was it. I don't search for hidden meaning in it, I fear it with all my heart, even though I know there is nothing more spiritual than suffering and that we are redeemed through it as through nothing else.

And yet... I don't want to suffer! If I were to have my way, I should throw my arms around all that is mine: people, children, lighted windows, snow in Moscow (that December snow so dear to my heart, blanketing back streets and graves before the turn of the year), all memories, all conversations, all smells (most of all those of my dacha, opened up again after the long winter, then the smell of lilies-of-the-valley, and then of raspberry jam) — I should throw my arms around it all, feeling cold shivers run up and down my spine from all these long-forgotten things washed up on the tight black waves of memory — throw my arms around it, dig the palms of my hands into the grass, press the whole weight of my body on top of it and refuse to let it go. Let me keep all that is mine, Lord, do not punish me with separation!

How did she endure? My soul-mate with the auburn plait, my coughing, tearful soul-mate, abandoned by love and consumed with remorse — how did she come through it all, treading that cold path which kept cracking and breaking up beneath her feet, until at its farthest point she died in her sleep, her cheek resting on cupped hands? Did the strength intended for both of us, the strength imprudently judged as sufficient for two, in fact all go to her?

The familiar house in the Arbat had become really run-down and battered (and that in just a year and a half, she thought). A young man in a shabby Red Army greatcoat came out of the front door, his eyes yellow and insolent-looking, the right side of his face twitching visibly.

'Where d'you think you're goin', citizen?' he bawled out cheerfully, barring her way with outspread arms.

'Do Nikolay Vasilyevich and Lydia Filitsyn live here?' she asked in a trembling voice.

'They might do. Who the hell are you, anyway?'

'Out of my way!' She made a sudden move for the door, but he pushed her back.

'Quite the little lady, aren't you! It ain't your place to raise your voice nowadays, you know. When someone asks who you are, you damn well answer 'em, and certainly don't order 'em out of the way! We don't have to make way for your sort any more — that was a mistake we're still payin' for today!'

The right half of his face was twitching convulsively, and his yellow eyes had become dark and full of malice. She was scared.

'Please let me pass, I beg you. I've come to see my sister. Lydia Filitsyn is my sister.'

'Oh, your sister!' The tic in his face suddenly stopped, and a jovial gleam came into his eyes. 'I wouldn't let you in to see your brother, but if it's your sister, be my guest.'

She suddenly felt her shoulders grasped by his enormous hairy hands.

'So you and I are gonna spend tonight under the same roof, eh?'

'Take your hands off her, Savely! Hands off, do you hear!'

Nikolay Vasilyevich stepped from the dark interior of the battered house, out into the snowflakes twirling and cavorting in the evening air. He looked much thinner, and he had acquired a tousled greying beard. With a gasp of recognition he held out his hands towards her.

'Liza, what a surprise! My dear!'

He was wearing a shapeless crumpled shirt of some sort, while draped over his shoulders was a red plaid that had worn into holes.

'Come inside, quickly now, come and see Lydia,' he said, putting one arm round her and picking up her puny little suitcase with the other. 'And don't let me see you around here!' he shouted abruptly at the man with the yellow eyes and twitching face, who turned and disappeared, melting into the dusk and snow.

Nikolay Vasilyevich stopped in the dark hallway and gave her a hug.

'How did you pluck up the courage to come, my dear? And what sort of journey have you had?'

'Don't even ask! More importantly, how is she?'

'Not well. But I'm hopeful. I shall pull her through, I won't let her go! Koko's with his aunts — Aglaya gets a professor's rations, so there's more food for him than at home, and Zinaida bakes bread. We barter our belongings for food and use the furniture for firewood. Lydia feels the cold badly — she has a lingering inflammation of the lungs on top of her heart trouble. You'll need to wash after your journey, Liza — don't be offended, but I can't let you in to see her as you are.'

She embraced her sister, horrified at the strange fragility of her body. She felt that if she pressed just a little harder, all the hot inflamed bones in her sister's arms, her elbows, her chest would snap without resistance. Lydia was on the wide leather sofa they had moved in from Nikolay Vasilyevich's study, lying under a cherry-coloured quilt covered with a sheet that was faded and yellowed from much washing. Each gazed into the other's

3—3317

tearful eyes that were so like her own, and neither was able to speak.

'How's Mummy? And Daddy?' Lydia managed to whisper at last. 'Are they alive? What about Grandma, Sasha, Nanny?'

'They're alive, they're alive, don't worry. I'll tell you everything. Only mind you don't excite yourself, or Nikolay will send me back out into the street again.'

Brushing Lydia's damp auburn plait against her own cheek, she told her the news from Tambov.

'...Daddy was just going off to sleep and Nanny had just finished her prayers, when there was this knocking at the door. It made the whole basement shake, it was so loud. Then these two men in leather jackets came in, unshaven and carrying revolvers, with a third man as well — God knows who he was, probably dragged in as an official witness. "Everyone get up!" they shouted. I said, "My father can't get up, he's ill." "We'll soon check that," they said. And of course, they found that Daddy couldn't get up and couldn't speak either. Within five minutes the three of them had turned the flat upside down. Not that there was really anything to turn upside down, the place was empty. Then they told Sasha: "Put your coat on, you're coming with us!" '

'Oh no!' cried Lydia, burying her face in her hands.

'Don't distress yourself, now, they let him go later. Someone had reported on him for being a former member of the Cadet party. After he was arrested Mummy wouldn't touch her food, Nanny spent all her time on her knees, praying, and Daddy just cried. He kept making signs to say it was all up with Sasha, crying all the time. And then I thought: what can I do, who can I turn to? Well anyway, a couple of weeks before Sasha was arrested this strange character had turned up at our house one morning. Small fellow, he was, slightly deformed, and he had a revolver too, like the others. Sasha, Nanny and Grandma weren't in, they'd gone off to barter for food. So then this fellow sits himself down at the table, takes off his cap and says to me: "I work for the Cheka, young miss citizen — I expect you've heard of our organization?" And his eyes had a crafty look to them, darting this way and that. Mummy was sitting at Daddy's feet — deathly pale, she was. "There's no need to be afraid," the fellow smirks. "I've got daughters too. Like you, they are, only a bit younger." I didn't say anything. "Show us your rings, miss citizen," he says. "What rings?" I ask. "Don't you play silly beggars with me, just get them trinkets out! Where do you keep 'em, wrapped up in a cloth, or in a box?"

'I couldn't move a muscle. I just sat there looking at him like an idiot. And then Mummy got up and without a word put this little casket down in front of him — the round pink one, you remember, with a cameo on the lid? His eyes lit up like a cat's in the dark. "Bloody hell," he said, "you must have been well-heeled, citizens! Blue sparklers, green ones, white ones — used to wear this little lot, did you?"

'He tipped them all out on the table and covered them with his cap. And then suddenly we heard Daddy making moaning noises, trying to say something. He'd pushed himself up on his pillows, and there were tears running down his face. He was making signs to us, using his left hand because his right hand's no good, he's almost lost the use of it.'

'What was he trying to say?' sobbed Lydia, hiding behind her auburn plaits and pulling the quilt over her face.

Only then did Liza catch sight of Nikolay Vasilyevich crouched down at the end of the leather sofa, making signs to her. He was silently shaking his fist and holding his other hand clapped to his mouth. She broke off in half-sentence. The cherry-red quilt in its yellowed cover, pulled over Lydia's head, began to flutter and tremble, and was shaken by little waves.

'Lydia, don't cry! What a stupid fool I was to tell you all that!'

The room with its small smoking stove was filled with a coughing that burst forth from beneath the auburn waves, from beneath the cherry-red quilt in its yellowed cover: a coughing as thick as the eye-stinging smoke itself, dark and rattling, with a squeezed remnant of breath huddled within.

'Lidochka, my darling, my sweet!'

That night they sat by the light of a primitive oil lamp in the room next to that where the smoky air, still seeming to preserve remnants of her painful fit of coughing, caused her damp auburn head to sway and spin as it lay deeply embedded in pillows, immersed in fitful sleep with all the dark eyelids, tears and light curls at the temples. Wrapped in his plaid (so worn through it resembled nothing more than a spider's web), Nikolay Vasilyevich was crushing pieces of greyish lump sugar on the broad palm of his hand, while Liza quietly continued her story.

'He said, "We'll share 'em out, miss citizen, seein' as I'm not a monster but a fighter for proletarian justice. You wore your jewels, now let my young beauties have a turn." And he actually divided Mummy's pink jewel casket into equal shares: "One ring for you, one for me; one necklace for you, one for me." After that he stood up, looking very pleased with himself, and shovelled the takings into his pocket. Then he tapped his holster with his finger and said, "Don't you be scared o' this contraption, ladies. We're only liquidatin' the class enemy in these parts, and you're classless types now — ordinary women, in other words..." And with that he went out, whistling. Oh yes, something else: when he got to the door he stopped for a moment, looked at Daddy and said, "Our 'pologies for troublin' you, citizen." '

'They're many-faced, Liza, like pagan gods,' said Nikolay Vasilyevich, his knife hovering in mid-air. 'One half laughing, the other crying. Two hands on their stomach, three on their chest and another one out of sight somewhere at the side. Damnation, one has to be so alert to what's going on all the time! There are too many different aspects involved, too many different things all thrown together into one vast rag-bag — from common-or-garden gangsterism, now sanctioned by law, to devil only knows what long-standing grievances and injustices. Throw in the cranky ideas of intellectuals, inflated egos, deprived childhoods, nervous disorders, and then...'

'Just a minute, dear, let me finish. When Sasha was arrested, I decided to try and find that man again. Grandma had a ring with a big diamond set in a rosette of smaller ones, which she never took off — it was her engagement ring from grandpapa, a really beautiful ring. We had to explain everything to her, and then we used soap to get the ring off, because after fifty years it was practically welded to her finger. Grandma didn't say a thing, just made the sign of the cross over me and gave me the ring, and I carried it around in my pocket for several days, searching for the Cheka man. Eventually I was lucky enough to spot him coming out of the entrance gates. Did you know they'd taken over the Aseyevs' house — the one with the white lions, do you remember?'

Nikolay Vasilyevich — sitting with his fist propped up against his grizzled unshaven cheek, and himself looking in the darkness like an enormous shaggy lion draped in a plaid — gazed at her sunken little face that was so grown-up now, so similar to Lydia's in the set of the eyes, feeling his heartbeat slow down or accelerate in time with her anxious pauses and bursts of growing agitation.

'I said to him, "Help my brother! He's not guilty of anything, he's not fighting against you. Please spare him!" And I held out the ring. He looked all round, and then — whoosh! — the ring had disappeared into his hand. I don't know how he went about it, or what he did, but a week later Sasha was set free.'

'Oh yes!' said Nikolay Vasilyevich, crouching in front of the stove and peering into its cold grey interior. 'What miracles we witness in our times! Instead of killing an innocent man they let him go, and we gasp in bewildered amazement, we rejoice at such a miracle! It's been less than two years, and yet already our brains have become so addled, so attuned to this unthinkable life that we adjust to its logic, trim our feelings to its monstrous rules and accept it as something inevitable, keeping any revulsion we might feel to ourselves. We should be tearing our hair out, shouting blue murder day and night, instead of which we put up with it all and rationalize it! What a paradox! Do you understand what I'm saying? We've been infected with these microbes, the disease has developed, and now we've already passed the acute crisis point when you hover between life and death, bathed in hot sweat, unaware of body or soul. We've survived that, and we don't even look particularly ill any more. But in fact the disease has gone into a further stage and become chronic. We are profoundly, incurably ill; and the worst of it is, we're infectious, a danger to others — first and foremost to our own children. But what's the point of talking about it all?'

'I understand,' she whispered, licking off some grains of sugar stuck to the knife. 'I know... I feel the same way.'

'Just to think!' Nikolay Vasilyevich went on hastily, throwing his large strong hands with fingers outspread into the air above the sorry-looking folds of his plaid, which was dislodged by the sudden movement. 'Just consider this: I spent my whole life dealing with the mentally ill, and I was used to that. But every evening I could shut the door on my last patient, empty my head of all the accumulated ravings I'd listened to during the day and return to a healthy life with its healthy difficulties and those deviations from the norm permitted by healthy logic. Mind you, I could see that in this life, too, people were sometimes on a knife-edge between sanity and insanity. If only you knew how many little eccentricities, how many actions and sayings were revealed to me, as a doctor, as being of a deeply pathological nature! Even so, observing the life around me may have left me feeling depressed or surprised, and I may have struggled to make sense of it all — but it didn't make my head spin, and life didn't seem one enormous nightmare as it does now. Patients were patients, and the rest were the rest. And then suddenly...'

He did not finish the sentence. Outside in the hall something fell over with a resounding crash and rolled along the floor, and a drunken tenor voice burst into song: 'Marching onwards, hup-two, hup-two! Keep in step with me, old chum!'

'Damned hooligan!' fumed Nikolay Vasilyevich, jumping from his seat. 'That wretched drug addict!'

Liza ran out after him, holding the oil lamp above her.

'Decided to come back, have you, you swine! If you don't shut that noise this instant, I'll thrash you within an inch of your life!' fumed Nikolay Vasilyevich, struggling to push Savely back into the street. Scarcely able to stay upright, the man in the snow-powdered overcoat dug his heels in and did his utmost to grab Nikolay Vasilyevich by the throat.

' 'at's what you think, pal,' he mumbled. 'Think you can put one over on me, do you? Ruddy bourgeois — should've 'ad your throat slit long ago! Bloody 'ospital louse!'

Nikolay Vasilyevich finally managed to get the better of him and threw him out into the street, into the dark swirls of driving snow.

'Cool off out there, you swine, and don't dare knock at this door before you've quietened down!'

There was a moan from Lydia's room.

'My poor darling!' murmured Nikolay Vasilyevich. His voice, which only a moment before had sounded so full-bodied and deep, with a hint of metal in the upper register, had become gentle beyond recognition. 'We've woken you up. Go back to sleep, Lydia, sleep now, my dearest.'

'Who exactly is this Savely?' asked Liza when they had returned to the abandoned stove.

Nikolay Vasilyevich threw his plaid over his shoulders. 'Savely,' he replied, 'is a citizen of the new order. Under the old order people like him would end up as criminals and be sent to labour camps, but under this new one they've become soldiers of the revolution. Six months ago he was invalided out of the army as a rather bad case of shell-shock; now he works on the railway and makes rabble-rousing speeches at meetings of domestic servants. In the evenings he hangs out with his cronies, who all distil their own hooch, and then he comes back here in the state you've just seen. Apart from that he's a cocaine addict — not just a commie, but a junkie too. I can't have him evicted, because he's a Hero of the Civil War, and I can't kill him either, much as I'd like to. All I can do is grin and bear it until he goes of his own accord or freezes to death in a snowdrift somewhere. Who knows, perhaps I underestimate the political danger he represents. For me he's no more than scum, dregs, riff-raff; but Lydia goes in panic fear of him: she sees him as some kind of supernatural being.'

He patted Liza on the shoulder and said, 'Off to bed with you now. And watch your step with Savely. He's no more than a fool when he's drunk, but when he's sober he can be a real swine. I shall be at the hospital all day tomorrow, so...'

Why do I yearn so for snow here in New England, where the honied air stretches like silk above the deserted beach with its wide-eyed seagulls and smell of rotting seaweed?

Is it because there, amidst snowdrifts piled high against ground-floor windows, something was first revealed to my soul? Is it because my soul can never forget that?

Snowdrifts. Ice-patterns on windows. Little snowcaps on the bare branches of trees.

'Are you prepared to work for the anti-illiteracy campaign?' the tall, wild-eyed man with a smoker's voice asked her.

Logs crackled in the stove. The man took a drag on his meagre roll-up, visibly turning a shade of green.

'Yes, I am.'

'You'll have women coming to you old enough to be your mother, your grandmother even. There'll be no making fun of them: you've to show them complete respect, understood?'

'Understood. What about teaching materials?'

He spread his hands helplessly.

'You might just as well ask for black pelerines!'

Today she had received her first allocation of rations, an unimaginable delight. There was soap, herring, a little grey flour, some vegetable oil, potatoes. As she walked along the narrow pathway trodden out in the snow, dragging her sack behind her, she suddenly heard a voice call her: 'Yelizaveta Alexandrovna, hello!'

She raised her head. In the darkening air, amidst sparsely falling, dry dancing snow stood the tall familiar figure of a man. The collar of his sheepskin jacket was turned up, and his shaggy fur hat was pulled down low on his forehead. But how familiar those dark, placid eyes were!

'Allow me rather belatedly to introduce myself: Konstantin Andreyevich Lopukhov. Your neighbour from Tambov, do you remember?'

Did she remember! She held out a frozen hand and said, 'How do you do, Konstantin Andreyevich. So you're in Moscow now?'

'Yes, I'm in the government service here.'

'Government service? You?'

They were standing in the way of other passers-by. 'Why

don't you come over to our place,' she said decisively. 'I'm staying at my sister's. Did you ever see my sister?'

'I saw you both through the window once. Do you remember, you came to Tambov together that summer just before the war began? A woman in a blue hat and a boy in a sailor suit...'

'Yes, that was Lydia. You won't recognize her now, she's changed a lot. Have I too?'

He looked at her closely, not answering her question. Was this really the same young girl who used to peep out at him surreptitiously from behind the door-curtains?

'Yes, you have, Liza,' he said simply. 'You've grown up.'

It is the morning of the sixth of May. Which year? I shall be starting school soon, so it must be 1958. The small windows of our wooden house open wide on to fluffy poplar down flying past outside, the chirping of sparrows, the ting-a-ling-ling of a tram in the street. The air smells of warm sun and fresh shoots of grass. The telephone rings, and my grandmother picks it up. She listens and turns pale, her free hand hanging at her side, her mouth open. Suddenly she thrusts the receiver into my father's hand and runs into the next room, slamming the door behind her. Through the door we hear first a moan, then a hoarse, choking 'Konstantin!', followed by screaming.

My father gathers me up into his arms and bounds down the stairs from the first floor to the street. Bright sunlight floods our little street, which is buried beneath drifts of poplar down and rent by the raucous chatter of young sparrows. As we walk along, he talks to me of other things, but I know the intonations of his voice too well and ask him, 'What's happened?'

He looks away.

'That was a phone call from the hospital. Your granddad has died.'


He sat in the cold little room of the battered house in the Arbat, straining to hear the voices on the other side of the door. Though somewhat muffled, Liza's animated voice easily outmatched the other, which was femininely smooth and low, with a strange whispering transparence to it, and a tendency to restrained coughing.

'Are you feeling any better today?'

'Perhaps a bit, I don't know.'

'Are you feeling hungry? I can cook something in a jiffy.'

'No, I'll have my medicine first. Nikolay popped in this afternoon with some milk, but I didn't drink it, I sent it to Koko.'

'That was silly! There's nothing wrong with Koko, thank God, but you need your milk.'

Half an hour later Liza put her dark face round the door, wrinkling her nose against the smoke from the stove.

'I'm sorry we were so long. Please come in, Lydia would like to see you.'

She was still a beautiful woman. Back then in the summer of 1914 he hadn't really managed to get a proper look at her.

Her auburn hair, shot through with gold at the temples, lay in tresses on the faded, yellowed pillowcase. Her dark eyes were surrounded by even darker rings, the imprint of infirmity and sleepless nights. Her dark eyes were all one soft engulfing darkness, like that of a warmed southern sky bereft of stars. Her pale hands picked at the folds of her cherry-red quilt.

Cautiously he sat down next to Liza on a blue bench by the stove.

'I'm pleased to meet you,' said Lydia. 'Liza says we were neighbours.'

'Yes, and then I was called up,' he said quietly, involuntarily moderating his voice to her whispered tones. 'In 1916 I was badly wounded and ended up in hospital for nearly a year. It was touch and go, but I pulled through eventually and was invalided out. I went to St Petersburg and was assigned to non-military duties, and then they sent me here, to Moscow. I've got a job as a kind of glorified clerk in the People's Commissariat of Education. Sometimes they make use of my legal training, but as a general rule I spend my days burrowing through papers like a tame rat.'

Liza snorted with amusement, then asked: 'Do you have any family left in Tambov?'

'My mother and two sisters. But it's a long time since I had any news from them. My closest friend — Stepan Obnovlensky, a colonel in the army medical service — left the country, he'd had enough. He did invite me to go with him, but I...'

'You what?' Liza's flushed face had moved closer to his. In the softly flame-tinted darkness her eyes flashed beneath the lynx-like tufts of her eyelashes.

His head was spinning slightly. Of course, he'd hardly eaten anything today, but it wasn't from that.

Where are we all, he thought, what's happening to us? It was dark in the room, with just the soft flame-light of the stove snatching from the darkness here and there warm fragments of this unique, condemned life: the familiar girl with her animated face and slightly muffled, questioning voice; the careworn auburn head on the faded pillow; and, beneath a starless sky, that dark ring of infirmity and sleepless nights...

His head spun. What's happening to me, he thought, where am I?

Outside the window snow was falling, blanketing the battered yellow house in the Arbat at whose heart flickered a weak flame, snatching from the darkness warm fragments of a life that was doomed, that was even now guttering away... Where are we all, he thought, what's happening to us?

'Lydia was so poorly that he didn't dare come to our house. Sometimes he'd meet me coming home from work, but it was bitterly cold that winter, and we didn't have the right footwear for walking around much. And then soon afterwards Lydia started to deteriorate.'

'Why was that?'

'Her heart couldn't cope any more. Apart from which, he... that man... turned up in Moscow. I think she just couldn't take it...'

She got up and, wearing Nikolay Vasilyevich's voluminous dressing-gown, with a grey scarf thrown over her head, took a few cautious steps through the unheated room. She'd decided she'd had enough of lying in bed.

She reached the window. Liza said the weather had been positively arctic the day before, yet today it was drizzling a sort of fine mist. It was the kind of damp morning that chilled you to the bone. She'd had enough of being ill, she must get up and get better. She must fetch Koko back from his aunts after all this time. Koko! How rarely she saw him! Her darling little boy...

Was she really to blame for the way everything had turned out? Yes, she was. At night sometimes, when feverish and coughing, she would imagine that all the horrors of this new life — the whole of this flame-swept, strife-driven, blood-soaked, starving land, in which all of them, including the boy with fair eyelashes whose piercing cries of: 'Mummy!' rang out in the mornings, and the boy at the very centre of their bleeding dismembered land, and the boy who had shared everything with them down to the last drop...

Merciful God! At this point, as the fever rose, her thoughts would invariably become confused, and with an effort of will she would struggle to marshal them into some sort of order again... And the boy she had once so shamefully abandoned, that child who had forgiven her, and who pretended not to understand anything, the boy... Her thoughts became confused, hopelessly confused... Perhaps everything happening to them now was nothing other than the retribution due to her? But how could that be? So much, all for a love she had been unable to overcome? And then... why involve so many people? Why should they all suffer if only she was to blame? Her thoughts in confusion, she would sink into a pitch darkness where only a child's fair eyelashes cast their striated pattern on her from within like thin streaks of winter light.

She was feeling better now, much calmer. She'd had enough of lying in bed, that was no way to throw off her illness. The coughing started up again. Carefully, trying not to provoke the stitch in her side, she drew breath. There was a knock at the door. It seemed there was no-one else in to answer it. Better not go, not in these godforsaken times, as Nikolay Vasilyevich would say.

The knocking was repeated, louder and more insistent this time. And, feeling her legs give way beneath her, she suddenly realized who it was. No, it couldn't be. How could it? Yet she knew it was. In the darkness that had fallen (although it was still only morning) she stumbled towards the door with her hands over her ears, trying to prevail against the deafening sound, forgotten since childhood, of forest grasshoppers chirping, which first grew louder and then died away as it was engulfed by the hot blood beating in her temples. No longer carried by her legs, which had simply ceased to exist, but walking on needles piercing her feet, she went out into the hallway, unfastened the latch and turned the key in the lock...

I can't see anything. Just a white blotch: the wan sun of my dreams, the slow fibrous pain of my stopping heart...

A white face covered in fine drops from the freezing January mist, nestling against the auburn head in the grey scarf.

'She told Nikolay Vasilyevich everything straight away that same night. He used to get back very late from the hospital. They slept in the room at the side, while I had what used to be his study. But I didn't hear a thing — I always went out like a light as soon as I hit the pillow...'

A light drizzle was falling outside, snow mixed with rain. Nikolay Vasilyevich stood his patched felt boots, which were wet, in front of the stove. They began to give off a pungent smell.

'Dammit, this won't do at all. I'm sorry, Lydia my dear, I'll put them out in the hall to dry. I just hope Savely doesn't pinch them.'

'Nikolay...'

He turned abruptly at the sound of her breaking voice.

'What is it, my dear, don't you feel well?'

My God, she thought, how am I going to tell him? What am I going to tell him? As if I didn't know — (How's Koko doing at his aunts'? And Mummy and Daddy? I just hope to God they're still alive!) — as if I didn't know what an awkward time it is for...

'Nikolay, he's here, in Moscow...'

What a stroke of good fortune: a pair of shoes, and practically new! He'd just happened to be passing a flea-market the day before and managed to snap them up there and then. They were a bit tight, but that was nothing, they'd soon wear in. Yes, he'd struck lucky all right, buying those shoes, for he had no decent footwear left at all. In ten or fifteen minutes Liza would finish teaching her class of old women, and they could go for a bit of a stroll, after which perhaps he'd be able to persuade her to call in on the Potapovs, where they could warm themselves up over a glass of tea. How simple everything was! It was only in the old days that he'd been able to afford the absurd luxury of complicating and dramatizing life. Back then, reflecting on the vanity of earthly existence, raging at the petty concerns of humankind or despairing at the impossibility of ever loving a woman, he'd never once paused to consider just how marvellous it was to drink strong sweet tea, to wear comfortable shoes, to sleep in a warm bed — marvellous not to feel oneself a cog in a relentless machine that had no sense or purpose, not to live in a country given over to fratricidal carnage, not to shake with abject fear at the thought of what the future held for you and those you loved...

Yes, he was certainly afraid of them. But how had it all come about? How exactly had a bunch of half-educated fanatics contrived to seize power and reduce the massive granite edifice of Russian life to rubble, grinding it all to a bloodstained dust? The French Revolution had shown the way... Yet even the French Revolution could never have envisaged *this*. This was all imbued with a uniquely Russian spirit: the murderous spirit of Pugachov, of Dostoyevskian devils... Lord, he thought, how little we appreciate what we have! If only some miracle could restore that relative prosperity he had once thought so bourgeois, so degrading and limiting — that glorious prosperity which would have allowed him to take Liza to the theatre, to accompany her — dark-eyed, pink from the cold, happy — into the dim red velvet shadows of their box, to hear the violins tuning up, to have ice cream in the buffet. Or to harness Dash one morning in fresh, burgeoning July and set off on a jaunt with his sisters in search of mushrooms, or drive out to a birthday celebration at somebody's dacha, with silly toasts and deafening fireworks... Lord, how little we appreciate Thy gifts, and how dearly we pay for our ingratitude!

'Konstantin Andreyevich...'

He started at the sound of her voice: that dear sweet voice, now husky from a slight cold.

What was he to do with this dark-eyed, olive-skinned, weary girl with the cold-muffled voice? What was he to do?

'Shall we walk together for a while, Liza? If you're not too bothered about getting cold, that is?'

It was growing dark. They walked through the snow-swathed city, the snow creaking beneath his new shoes.

'I hope you'll understand,' she said, turning her glowing face, sad and wide-eyed, towards him, 'but I can't stay too long, because things are so difficult with Lydia. Nikolay Vasilyevich insists on her going into hospital, but she doesn't want to — she thinks she'll die straight away if she does, and even Nikolay Vasilyevich is afraid she might catch typhoid fever there. She keeps asking us to bring Koko to her, but he's not too well himself at the moment, running a temperature, and we're afraid to tell her because she'll convince herself something even worse has happened to him. Oh dear, it's all so difficult!'

'Liza, my dear,' he said, taking her gently by the arm and turning her to face him. 'Liza, do you trust me?'

'Yes, of course.' Her wet eyes were open wide as they gazed at him questioningly above the white of her collar, above the white snow of that terrible winter of 1919 which had brought them so close together. 'Of course. Lydia, Nikolay Vasilyevich and you are the only people I have here.'

'In that case,' he continued, suddenly embarrassed, and grasping her arm more firmly, 'let me be yours to command, yours entirely and for all time. I'm sorry if that sounds awfully pompous.'

She did not say thank you. She did not say thank you, but with pounding heart, her frozen hands still inside the bedraggled reddish-brown fur of her muff, stood on tiptoe, held her cold face to his and kissed him firmly on the lips.

'Why do you think I said to you that in a sense our marriage was a matter of pure chance? What if we'd never met that winter? What if he hadn't been so affected by Lydia's beauty, and by her illness? He told me himself that when he saw her like that, already marked out by death, his heart turned over. So I wasn't really in the picture at all to start with, just bathing in reflected glory. He couldn't leave us after that. For him the two of us had become — she in the final weeks of her life, I with my constant colds, my hunger, my frightful appearance — little oases of an agreeable, normal way of life, to which he felt drawn by a kind of inner affinity.'

Not far from her house they slowed down as if by common accord. The snow had stopped, and far above their heads the depths of space had opened up, quivering with unforeseen stars.

'You know,' she said, looking up into his face, which appeared younger and more serene now, 'I've never been able to make up my mind whether I'm religious or not. When I lift my head and see stars and emptiness, I ask myself: is there a God out there or not? And I don't know the answer. What do you think?'

'I think God is there all the time, everywhere and in everything — like carbon. And the longer I live, the more closely I feel His presence. Without Him everything falls apart, both spiritually and materially. Yet I can't explain this sensation I have in words: I just feel it, that's all.'

She suddenly remembered Alexander and their conversation about death in Nikitsky Boulevard. Had it really been so long ago? It had — nearly five years! And was she really never going to see him again? What was it he'd said? 'I'll come back from the front, and then we'll get married. You know, I had our future life together mapped out a long time ago.' But he was gone, he didn't exist anywhere now.

Involuntarily she had turned from him, become distant. As

if sensing the drift of her thought, he said, 'I must tell you all about myself soon. After all, we hardly know each other.'

She would often emphasize her atheism, dismissing any questions of mine by saying, 'How should I know what happens then? When we kick the bucket we'll see.' And then suddenly...

No longer merely old, she had in the space of some six months grown positively ancient. Yellow-looking, her eyes dull and senseless, her feet so swollen that no slippers fitted her any more, she would sit in the large red armchair by the window, her small hands — still dark, though wrinkled — leafing through the crumbling pages of a velvet-bound prayer-book inscribed on the first page with her maiden initials. Not reading the prayer-book, she would just hold it and stroke it with her trembling hands, gazing at it with unmoving eyes.

I am quite clear in my memory that never before — neither in my childhood nor later on — had she ever touched this battered little book, whose very survival must be counted a miracle. Now there would be an icon print, cut out of some book or magazine, propped up against the table lamp next to a half-full cup of tea and an old watch.

In the evenings she would lie sunk in the physical hopelessness of her approaching end, already for some time now practically speechless, practically bereft of all reaction to the life around her; and I would hear, wrung from her blackened lips, the whispered, sibilant plea:

'Lord receive me. I am ready to come to Thee, o Lord.'

'Swine! Pervert! Cocaine addict!' she screamed, and her

delicate fists pummelled frantically at the repulsive body which lay pinning her to the floor.

Savely, in puttees and unbuttoned military tunic, smacked his lips, breathing into her face a mixture of alcohol fumes and something else with a sweetish smell reminiscent of cheap ground rice. His hairy hands squeezed at her neck and breast.

'Come on now, Liza! 'Ere, listen to what I'll give you, Lizzie!' His hot wet lips battened on her cheeks. 'Just a quick one, eh Lizzie?'

Managing to free a hand, she landed a punch on the fleshy red face with its sweaty creases, furrows and pock-marks. She felt she was losing consciousness. The reek of cheap rice powder and alcohol fumes filled her with nausea, and she nearly vomited. What good would it do to shout for help? There was only Lydia at home, and she was ill.

'Come on, just the once,' wheezed Savely, reeling drunkenly as he jerked her up from the floor.

And then, plaintively, she called in a thin high-pitched voice: 'Lydia!' Yet even before her plaintive cry had died away, Lydia burst out of the living room into the hallway, wearing Nikolay Vasilyevich's voluminous dressing-gown and holding up a candle-end to illuminate the darkness. Keeping the candle in one hand, she used the other, free hand and her bare feet to belabour the shaggy, alcohol-reeking, half-naked animal that had her sister clutched in its hairy paws.

Now blows rained down from three dark-skinned, ringless fists, white-knuckled with tension, as the two of them set about him, grunting with the effort and muttering every oath known to them, the whole extravagant spectacle — inspiring horror and hysterical laughter in equal measure — lit by the guttering candle held aloft and to one side of the action.

So they worked away at him with their weak, white-knuckled fists, while he — dumbfounded, scarcely able to stay upright — struggled to avert his fleshy red face with its wet lips, its furrows and pock-marks.

Where did they find the strength — one of them dying, the other worn to a shadow, plagued with colds and scarcely able to stay on her feet from exhaustion — the ferocious strength of their onslaught on this creature in the unbuttoned tunic, weakened by alcohol and cocaine as he was? It was as if they sought to vent on him all their pent-up feelings of detestation (now suddenly released from the constraints of feminine modesty) for what was happening around them, singling him out as the target of their spontaneous protest against the blind, ruthless, infamous manner in which their lives had been overturned and trampled underfoot.

Once upon a time they had been girls in neatly ironed dresses who spoke three languages, who thanked their parents with an unforced curtsey after dinner, whose delicate transparent fingers struggled to master intricate scales; and then, suddenly, all this had become no more than a memory, had turned to smoke and ashes. They had become women, brutalized by animal fear and pain and haunted by nightmares. In one of them the boy with fair eyelashes whose deafening cries of: 'Mummy!' rang out in the mornings would curl up and fall asleep for ever from cold and hunger in the freezing apartment of his aunts, and she would run to him in her dream through air and snow, moving as fast as she could on unresponsive legs that had turned to jelly, to find him no longer alive. In another nightmare, which was common to both of them and recurred with diabolical frequency, the dark basement of their house in Dvoryanskaya Street would be swarming with rats: unshaven, nicotine-stained rats with pistols and little yellow teeth that chattered rapaciously as they gnawed at the remains of the two sisters' grandmother, nanny and paralysed father, who were all dressed in the same padded jackets.

Now they were laying into one of these rats for all they were worth. When eventually it dragged itself off to its lair, wheezing and spitting blood, they returned to their room, where the cherry-red quilt still lay where it had slipped to the floor, and the two of them fell about helpless with laughter, wiping tears from their eyes.

This was how Nikolay Vasilyevich found them when he returned from the hospital.

'What's been going on?' he asked, averting his eyes as they met Lydia's. It was only a couple of weeks since the past he had thought dead and buried had reared its head again. That would have to happen just now, when she was so ill! He knew that his wife always told him the truth: if she said that had been the only visit, then it was, and *he* hadn't been back again. But what of the future? Heavens above, was there really any point speculating about that? The main thing was for her to get better, and it was he — the father of her child — whom she needed if she was to be saved.

Must I really spend the rest of my life running away from phantoms, he thought. *He* is in Moscow... How long can I go on tormenting myself with suspicions? But merciful God, it hurts so, it hurts so...

Swallowing back the lump in his throat, Nikolay Vasilyevich

forced himself to look her calmly in the face and kissed the damp auburn hair at the back of her head.

'Listen to this! Just leave the kasha for now, I'll warm it up in a minute.' Liza, her face flushed, put her arms round his neck. 'When I came home and opened the door, Savely was there — he threw himself at me like a tiger. I kept hitting the swine, but I could feel that it was all over, my strength was giving out. And then Lydia came flying out of the room, barefoot and with your dressing-gown on, like a Roman toga! She could just have been... what was her name: the goddess of vengeance! Anyway, she started laying into him with hands and feet. Where in heaven's name did she learn to fight like that? Spitting at him, punching him with her fists — you wouldn't have believed your eyes! And then, taking advantage of Lydia's help, I knee him in the stomach. He doubles up like a jack-knife, and just then Lydia brings her fist down on his neck. On top of which he's got hot wax dripping down on him! "Oh, you bitches!" he howls, and starts backing away, trying to escape to his room. But we wouldn't let him go, we just went on beating and scratching him, cursing at him all the time. I tell you, Kolya, you should have heard some of the names we called him!'

'What sort of names?' asked Nikolay Vasilyevich with a guarded smile.

'What sort?' she laughed gleefully. 'The sort you'll hear if you behave badly enough!'

It was a memorable evening. Who says we never enjoy dazzling little victories of this nature?

It was a memorable evening, because the day before they had sawn up the walnut sofa, and now the legs with their ornately carved clusters of grapes were crackling away merrily in the stove, lighting up the almost empty room with the cherry-red quilt at its centre and the worn blue velvet of the little bench next to the fire itself. Revelling in the silky red and velvet blue, the walnut blaze enveloping the clusters of grapes cast a friendly glow on their warmed faces, and her auburn tresses, shot through with gold at the temple, breathed deeply and evenly.

'Nikolay, don't tell me those are raisins!'

'Just try them if you don't believe it. I was called out today to the home of a big Party boss whose mother-in-law's hallucinating after typhoid fever. She talks to her dead husband at nights: "You'd best join the Bolsheviks, Ivan, or if you don't watch out they'll be signing you up behind your back." That sort of thing, and crying too — a pretty familiar disorder. Anyway, they paid me handsomely for my visit.'

Before their astonished eyes on the cherry-red quilt appeared a loaf of white bread, a piece of amber-yellow butter in grease-proof paper, some delicately scented soap and a bag of small firm raisins.

It was a memorable evening. Best of all, she was hardly coughing, and felt less feverish than usual.

Who says that women unhappy in love are less attached to life than anyone else? How wide of the mark that is! On the contrary: caught in their predicament, they feel a particular need to prolong their physical existence, for each day successfully negotiated proves that the error committed or sin embraced — or that tormented, illicit, burning affair that goes under the name of both sin and love — does not after all merit death.

She wanted to live; and that evening the desire to live was stronger than ever.

At night Nikolay Vasilyevich and Liza would take it in turns to do the washing. Today it was Nikolay Vasilyevich's turn.

'Go to sleep, Lydia,' he said, and tiptoed out of the room.

She closed her eyes and straight away saw Koko. She saw him as he had been when he first came into the world. 'There we are now, sonny, there, let's come and show you to Mummy,' the kindly black-haired midwife had crooned in a sing-song voice, holding a tightly swathed bundle in front of her face. Amidst a froth of linen she saw his tiny yellow forehead creased in a frown, his trembling fair eyelashes. Immediately this vision gave way to the nightmares which had become routine of late. She was walking through dense green forest fragrant with lilies of the valley and unripened wild strawberries, carrying him in her arms. He was tightly swaddled as before, but now his milky eyes — the colour of the morning sky or sea — were open. Suddenly she felt something sting her on the leg. With a scream she put the bundle down on the grass and lifted the flounces of her long checked dress with both hands. A dull black mark was spreading across her leg. She held a plantain to it and blew on it. Then she heard a sudden rustling sound behind her back, and on turning round saw an empty space in the thick green grass: the bundle with the milky-blue open eyes had gone.

She was woken by her own coughing. It spilled from her like a heavy fall of brown snow: a hot, gut-wrenching flux, finely veined with pink blood.


I was twenty-one, and I was expecting a baby. The thought of it embarrassed me: my childish mentality still lagged a long way behind life. And suddenly something happened. I had never imagined the birth would go other than smoothly, but in fact I went into labour prematurely. I was in a very bad way and had to be rushed to the operating theatre, with several doctors exchanging brief anxious phrases as they hurried along beside the trolley on which I lay. In the operating theatre, while they were taking my blood pressure and giving me an injection, I asked the senior surgeon, who smelled of eau de cologne and looked like a pirate: 'Doctor, what's going to happen to me?'

After a brief pause he replied, 'We're going to save your life.' And bending closer to my face, he repeated, '*Your* life, you understand?'

'But...' I mumbled, feeling the blood suddenly rush to my head, 'I mean the baby...'

And then my body, laid out on the trolley in readiness for the operation, and the soul clinging so tenaciously to it, felt the laceration of words as cold and sharp as a razor: 'Forget about the baby. You're the one we're going to save.'

Straight after this I started seeing green and yellow rings popping up and spinning in front of my eyes, and in between them suddenly became aware of the Black Sea, deep and breathing noisily, and I had sunk to the bottom, powerless to resist.

First there was a searing pain in my abdomen and legs, obliquely smothered by a heavy weight of ice in a rubber hot-water bottle. Then, overcoming the agonizing weight of pain, I floated up from the bottom of the noisily breathing Black Sea, trying to reach out to the pirate in the white smock who stood, swarthy and smelling of eau de cologne, with his back to the strangely high and absolutely level bed which for me had now replaced the undulating sea floor.

The pirate bent down close to my burning face.

'Are you awake? Well done! You've had a little boy, do you understand? A little boy!'

Then for six or seven days and nights I lay burning up with fever while they struggled to save my baby as he hovered between life and death. A nurse who was on duty in the baby ward on the fourth night later told me that at about two in the morning they ran out of oxygen: he turned blue and began to suffocate, and the fine thread linking his life with mine seemed about to snap. This same nurse — whose name I do not know, but to whom I shall be eternally grateful — ran to another wing of the hospital and managed to get hold of another oxygen pack; and then my four-day-old son with his fair eyelashes and the rubber tag round his wrist revived.

After another couple of days I was moved to the second floor for the final stages of treatment, while he was due to be sent to a special clinic for premature babies.

Wearing a frightful hospital gown with tapes and with my hair let down, I sat dangling my legs from the bed, watching the door. A nurse (not the one who had got the oxygen pack, but another one who went with the babies from the maternity hospital to the clinic) had promised to bring him to me for a moment before they left. They hadn't shown him to me at all up to then, and my anxiety that something had happened and they were hiding it from me had grown with each passing day. The door opened, and a short, rotund woman came striding resolutely towards me. Slung from her shoulders were two bundles tightly swathed in grey hospital blankets with a large monogram stamped in the middle.

'There you are, have a look, dearie, only quickly now — I'm breaking all the rules by showing him to you. Yours must be this one on the left here.'

Without getting up from the bed I stretched out towards the grey bundle with its official monogram and peered at the almost soundlessly breathing contents. There in that rough grey recess, which had begun to swim before my eyes, lay my son, asleep, his scarcely visible fair eyelashes trembling beneath his brown, frowning little forehead.

Oh, how my soul recognized him! How it unfurled its sharp fettered wings and, weeping, beat against the cage of my ribs!

'That's it, dearie, that's all we've time for. You'll start feeding him in a couple of weeks, and then you'll be able to look at him as much as you like.'

She disappeared again through the door. Women in the other beds were staring at me inquisitively. I pulled my loosely hanging hair over my burning face to hide behind, and turned away.

That night when everyone on the second floor was asleep, as the penetrating cries and moans of women in labour drifted up from the first floor, I lay with my eyes fixed on a bright glittering star high above the crowns of some poplars, making no attempt to wipe away the tears streaming down my face and soaking the collar of my hospital night gown, just remembering.

'My dear, darling daughters, I hope that at least this letter will reach you, although I know you will find the news it contains unbearably painful. Daddy has passed away; we laid him to rest a few days ago. He had a peaceful end and knew no pain, although his perception was clouded to some extent. The doctor (Fyodor

Matveyevich, God bless him) stayed with him almost constantly, as we all did too. Weep for him, my dears, as we weep for him here; yet understand that for him death came as a deliverance from all the horrors that brought his illness on in the first place. It doesn't do to rail against God: His decisions, as always, are wiser and more merciful than our poor minds can ever hope to grasp. That, if you remember, is what I have always believed, both in better times and now, when at times one cannot even bring oneself to look at what is happening.

'We just about manage to get by. Nanny shows greater strength and resilience than any of us: she searches out food, cooks, and has taught herself to make unusually hard-wearing shoes by sewing rags together. We should simply not have survived without her. Sasha is working as a mechanic on the railways at present, but God alone knows how long he'll be able to hang on to his job there. I pray to the Lord to protect him, to make things turn out all right somehow. He keeps on at me about conscience, saying that all this has been visited on us as retribution for the well-fed, prosperous lives we led, and that he's quite prepared to accept suffering for our former sins.

'But then I think: did we really sin all that much? Your father was never idle and did a lot to help people in a quite unselfish way, and when I brought you up I tried to foster in you the very highest ideals and a strong sense of conscience. And is anything solved after all by spilling blood? My darling daughters, I don't know how things are with you in Moscow, but here people are shot on the slightest denunciation, without any reason or justification whatever. Whole groups are carted off to Klyucharevo and buried there in mass graves. Last week they shot Volodya

Tikhomirov (the husband of your friend Nadya Subbotina, Liza).
Someone had informed on him for being an officer in the White
Army, which was true. But when Nadya had twins he'd come
back to see them against all the odds, risking life and limb, and
that was where they arrested him. Nadya is a pitiful sight. Nanny
went to see them and came back in tears. Nadya's milk has dried
up — how will her babies survive?

'My dear daughters, forgive me for writing such a sad letter.
I am crying myself even as I write. But what can one do? These
were bad times for me to bring you into the world. My only wish
is to see you both alive and well, not forgetting Nikolay Vasilyevich
and my darling Koko. Then I shall be able, as Nanny says, to go
to my rest.

'I bless you, my dears, my precious ones, and send my most
tender, heartfelt kisses. Mummy.'

It was nice and warm in the Potapovs' flat. They had real
firewood burning in their stove, and on the table were white cups
with a dark-blue flower pattern, jam in an ornately scalloped crystal
dish and thinly-cut slices of white bread.

The previous day he had said to her, 'Liza, we're going to
visit an old friend of mine. Don't be surprised at all the things
you see there. Potapov enjoys a special relationship with the
Bolsheviks: they need him, because he's a scientist of world repute.
They've got rid of plenty of those so far, and they'll get rid of
even more, but God willing he'll manage to hold on longer than
the rest. They use him for the kind of work where he's the leader
in his field. Apart from which, he's no hero: he just wants to live,
and he's concerned for his family. The students at the university

idolize him — that's the charisma of genius for you. I said I'd take you there. Only... You won't be offended?..'

'What?'

'What do you have to wear?'

'To wear?' she said, colouring.

'Liza, please don't be offended! You'd look great in a crow's nest for a hat, but it's just that I'd like us to spend an evening with friends the way we used to, for old times' sake. To do things in style, if you see what I mean.'


Dressed only in her petticoat, she stood hunched up against the cold in the middle of the room, while Lydia with patches of hectic red on her cheeks quietly issued instructions.

'Have a look at my lilac dress. Yes, that's the one. Try it on. Now turn around.'

Standing in the frozen gloom in front of a yellowish ice-like fragment of mirror, she carefully slipped the rustling lilac dress over her head.

'It's a bit big,' whispered Lydia. 'Mouse, mouse, said the elephant, why are you so small?'

Liza remembered the joke. 'Because I've been ill,' she laughed.

Holding her heart, her sister took a breath. 'It's not really too big for you. Can you find my black shawl with the flower on it?'

'Your shawl? You'll have me looking like a gypsy!' With a shock she remembered how once, a hundred years ago, Musya had hissed in her ear: 'Lopukhov has a gypsy woman as a mistress!'

'Never mind,' said Lydia, holding her heart. 'Put the shawl on.'

She looked searchingly in the mirror and gave herself a smile. Round dimples appeared in her cheeks. The elegant lilac dress, plucked from the recesses of a life now gone for ever, framed her slim olive-coloured neck in a smooth semicircle and hung from her in casual folds. She draped the black shawl with the glistening flower over her shoulders. It all looked beautiful: the warm olive tones of her young skin; the dark gleam of her delighted eyes beneath thick eyelashes; the black flower, its velvety petals open, on her left shoulder.

'And now the ring,' said Lydia quietly, still holding her heart. 'What ring?'

'My diamond ring. I've still got it. Down there under the encyclopedia, in a little box — open it, take it out.'

Potapov's face was old and careworn, his chin blue-shadowed from meticulous shaving. His wife Yelena Sergeyevna was small and awkward, with shy transparent eyes. She attended to her guests with delicate solicitude. One could see she felt uncomfortable about the thinly sliced bread in the wicker basket, the plum jam, the hot fluffy omelettes which she brought in on dark-blue and white plates.

Lydia's ring sparkled radiantly. They sat side by side, and every now and then the lilac silk of her sleeve brushed against his grey pinstripe jacket of pre-war cut.

All of this — the fluffy light omelettes, his white shirt, Lydia's dazzling ring — was a vision from that life now gone forever. She felt she had only to shake her head for it all to disappear.

'You may laugh at what I'm about to say,' Potapov said emphatically with a frown on his face, 'but it all began with

Pechorin. Onegin was a decent fellow. Is it really so important that he didn't know what to do with his life? That's neither here nor there, for heaven's sake! The main thing is, he was a genuine human being, and morally aware. After killing Lensky he became mentally disturbed — so disturbed, in fact, that he literally started seeing things. You remember: "He left his village, seeking only to flee its woods and meadows lonely, where bloodstained visions of his friend had dogged his footsteps without end." What is that if not an illness, a mental disorder? Pechorin on the other hand was a depraved youth, a cold-blooded juvenile who, still wet behind the ears, flattered himself that the world was unworthy of him. What was his reaction on seeing the bloodstained corpse of Grushnitsky, whom he'd just killed, lying in a cleft of the rock face? "Involuntarily I shut my eyes." Well, bully for him! Now I don't presume to judge what it was that Byron got his kicks from — I'll leave that for the English to sort out. All I know is that on Russian soil rejection of God and affirmation of self have led to catastrophic results.'

'Do you think it all began with the rejection of God?' asked Liza timidly. 'I remember my father saying the same when all this first happened.'

'Yes, Lizaveta Alexandrovna, yes indeed, my dear. And the pattern of events is tiresomely simple, from the middle of the last century to the dark days we're living through now. How did it all start? To put it in simple terms, I'd say it all started with half-educated youths still wet behind the ears taking exception to the world around them — youths with no soul who had never really experienced anything in their snivelling lives. They found this world "bourgeois", and they proposed to do away with it. The divine will was subjected to re-evaluation. These youths turned up their noses at life as it is, they took exception to "the waters' brilliant azure", to "the sunlight's golden rays". And just mark those words: azure, sunlight! All his Pechorinesque conceits notwithstanding, Lermontov remained essentially a poet of genius, and the pen of a poet is invariably guided by God: in poetry as a rule things receive their precise designations, everything is in its proper place, wouldn't you agree? Anyway, you see, these youths felt they'd like a bit of a storm. A storm, you see, might settle their over-excited minds. And so they got to work: spouting hot air, sharpening axes to use on old women, teaching people how to turn themselves from human beings into machines (I refer to that Chernyshevsky) — and now here they are, hoist with their own petard. Yes, the devil can always find work to do. Do you find the azure sky not to your liking, gentlemen? Are you bored by sunshine? How about a nice ride in a machine-gun cart through a famine-struck village so you can feast your eyes on living skeletons? Jump in, Mr Pechorin, I'll take you for a nice brisk joy-ride! Your wish has been granted — here's that storm you called for!'

Konstantin shuddered. What the old man with the blue-shadowed chin had been saying applied to him as well. Liza sat listening, her mouth half-open. How true that was about the storm.

'Mitya, why upset them like that, my dear?' Yelena Sergeyevna reproached her husband gently. 'Surely there are other things we can talk about?'

'Lena,' said Potapov, his face becoming tense, 'I'm a sick man, and a sick man's only topic of conversation is illness. The way I live now means having to shoulder a heavy burden of sin: I eat the devil's bread and drink the devil's tea, sweetened with the devil's sugar. That time the Cheka kept me in custody for ten days I came out like putty in their hands, or have you forgotten?'

'Do you feel remorse?' The words stuck in Liza's throat, and she coughed.

'Remorse?' His eyelids fluttered. 'How can I feel remorse? I've saved my dear wife and two daughters from the privations of cold and hunger. Is it humanly possible to know you have it in your power to help your loved ones, and then refuse to do so? No, I don't feel remorse; but my heart still grieves for what I've done.'

It had stopped snowing, and the sky was sprinkled with bright winter stars. Deep snowdrifts thinly encrusted with ice loomed white before them. There was not a soul in sight as they walked down Nikitsky Boulevard, an incongruous couple in this time of civil war: she with cheeks flushed from the recent warmth and excitement, wearing a white knitted headscarf which accentuated her dark hair and thick dark eyelashes; and he, broad-shouldered, in a sheepskin jacket unbuttoned to reveal an impeccable white starched shirt and pinstripe suit of pre-war cut.

'Liza,' he said quietly, 'Liza, my dear, Potapov's absolutely right about one thing: in this crazy world hurtling out of control like a train without a driver the most important thing is to love and be loved — to feel every day that someone needs you, that you are responsible before God Himself for someone dear to you. This feeling of responsibility is our only salvation. It's how a mother feels towards her child: it transcends everything else, it's absolutely fundamental. Yet in my egoism (that confounded egoism!) I never dreamed that this simple truth would in the end be revealed to me, and at such a heavy price. My precious ego had to be shaken to its foundations before the ground could be knocked away from under my feet and I could say, looking at you, that I...'

He faltered, catching his breath. They stopped. There they stood in the white snow of deserted Nikitsky Boulevard, beneath a clear starlit sky, in that terrible winter of 1919 — these two who gave life to my mother and predetermined my own distant unborn life: the woman in the lilac silk dress that hung down in folds from beneath her short coat, and the broad-shouldered man in the starched white shirt.

There they stood and remained, unmoving, unheeding...

'I love you and ask you to be my wife,' he said in a whisper, removing his hat to bare his thick head of hair to the starlit sky casting its blessing on them from above. 'I promise you, Liza, that my whole life will belong to you, that I shall devote every ounce of strength in my body to keeping you and any children we may have from harm. My whole life, do you hear? Every ounce of strength.'

It was decided to wait until spring. 'We're going to get married in the spring,' Konstantin announced. Nikolay Vasilyevich felt she would be up and about again by then. The sun would help. Her breathing would improve in the spring.

Her birthday, the sixteenth of February, was a mild, springlike day. In the morning Aglaya came with Koko. He had grown during the winter; now with a serious expression he looked at his mother from beneath his fair eyelashes, evidently trying to think of something to say to her. She took his hand in both of hers.

'He won't read,' Aglaya complained in her deep voice. 'A proper little ignoramus he's growing into. You wait and see, though, Mummy'll take you in hand — when it gets a bit warmer you must come and read aloud to her.'

Koko gave an embarrassed smile, taking on a startling resemblance to Nikolay Vasilyevich. What bliss it was just to look at him! Without letting go of his hand she cautiously dabbed the corner of one eye against the pillow. When they had gone, she gazed at the two little puddles of melted snow left on the floor by the sofa, trying not to cough. One moment her heart would be beating wildly, as if struggling to free itself from her body, then it would falter and die away as if ceasing to exist.

'Will he remember what day it is today — the sixteenth of February? Must I keep having these thoughts? After all, hasn't it been four years now — four years in which everything's been turned on its head, the past torn up by its roots! How can I even have such thoughts, lying here bedridden as I have for nearly three months now? Lord, help me to conquer them! And yet... will he remember what day it is today — the sixteenth of February?'

'I baked a tart with rye flour, and Konstantin brought all sorts of goodies from the Potapovs: eggs, butter, fruit drops. She got out of bed and got dressed, and we laid the table and waited for Nikolay Vasilyevich to come home from the hospital. I plaited her hair and garlanded the plait round her head the way our nanny used to have it when we were children. Lydia was in a state of nerves — it seemed to me it was all she could do to keep from crying. Of course, she was waiting for him to turn up, and by evening she was quite distraught that he hadn't. I suppose she thought he'd come during the day when Kolya and I weren't there, but he didn't. At the time I was completely preoccupied with my own relationship with my fiance, — which was really something out of this world, in spite of everything! — so I was far too wrapped up in myself to sense what was happening with her. Suddenly there was a knock at the door. Konstantin went to see who it was and came back with *him*...'

When he entered that room with the cherry-red quilt, the crackling stove, the round rye-flour tart, and saw the terrible pallor flooding her face beneath its garland of auburn hair, it may well be that he regretted coming.

Liza froze as she was, a knife in her hand, her mouth half-open.

'I've come to wish you happy birthday, Lydia, and a speedy recovery, and, well...'

He put something down on the table, looking embarrassed. Her face went even paler, the shadows beneath her eyes deepening to an almost jet-black intensity.

'That was when I realized just how much she loved him, Anya, seeing it for myself like that. The way she looked at him, spellbound — you should have seen her eyes! How she managed to keep her composure I can't imagine. She asked him to sit down...'

He was certainly embarrassed. The stove roared and crackled. Without rising from the blue velvet bench, she held out an almost transparent hand.

'Thank you for coming. This is my sister, Liza, and this is Konstantin Andreyevich Lopukhov, who was our neighbour in Tambov.'

He bowed without taking his eyes off her.

'Sit down,' she smiled. 'Would you like some tart?' Helplessly she smiled again. 'I'm so glad you came!'

'Anya, if only you could have seen how she looked at him! All the different emotions on her face... Pain... happinesss... And love — my God, so much love, so much light!'

The conversation, which had got off to an awkward start, kept foundering in lengthy pauses and having to be artificially revived. Hesitantly Liza reached out to the little package he had brought.

'May I? What is it?'

She undid the package. On the grey wrapping paper lay a large chunk of dark-golden honeycomb. Gleaming gently, it gave off a faintly bitter aroma.

'That's quite amazing! How did you come across that?'

He shrugged his shoulders in embarrassment. 'Just by chance, really.'

'This'll do your cough good, Lydia.'

'It'll do everyone good,' Lydia corrected her. 'Come on, let's try it.'

'*I did taste but a little honey with the end of the rod that is in my hand, and, lo, I must die.*'

She started. 'Where does that come from?'

'From the Bible,' he said with a grin. 'First Book of Kings.'

'And then Konstantin added: "Lermontov took those words as the epitaph to *Mtsyri*, which, as you'll recall, is about a Chechen boy who finds himself in a Georgian monastery. The honey stands for freedom: he tries it, and pays for it with his life." But Lydia interrupted him: "He pays with his life for a delusion, not for freedom. Surely the point is that throughout those three days when he thinks he's running away to his own country, he's actually just been circling round and round the monastery, where nobody was forcing him to stay anyway — where they'd saved his life, in fact..." '

The front door was hurriedly slammed to, and Nikolay Vasilyevich appeared in the room. She rose impulsively from the blue velvet bench. For a few seconds Nikolay Vasilyevich looked over the top of her head, gazing somewhere above the garlanded auburn hair with its heavy strands of gold. Then he said calmly, 'I'm a bit late. Forgive me, Lydia my dear. We had a lot of new patients coming in this evening, and then I was stopped by a patrol in Skatertny Lane.'

'Had they met before?'
'Of course. I don't think they'd seen each other since Lydia confessed all to Nikolay Vasilyevich. But of course, they'd met before that.'

Nikolay Vasilyevich did not look at anyone apart from Lydia. In fact he was not even really looking at her, just at her garlanded auburn hair with its strands of gold. His thoughts seemed elsewhere as he sat, ponderous, his greying hair dishevelled. He declined the honey, saying, 'It's too sweet, I've gone off that sort of thing,' but polished off a piece of Liza's tart with gusto and drank two cups of hot water.

Then he said in a calm voice, 'One of the children in my care died at the hospital today. A girl — eleven years old, I don't know exactly. A couple of hours before she died one of the nurses went to attend to her and saw she was putting on her scarf. The nurse asked her: "Why are you doing that?" and the girl said: "I want the dear Lord to see me looking pretty." Now there's a thing...'

He fell silent, and nobody else spoke. Lydia hung her head.

'Well, I seem to have cast a gloom over the proceedings,' he said, and kissed Lydia's hand. 'Forgive me, Lydia my dear; it's your birthday, and here am I telling stories like that... But here's another, a funny one this time. On my way home I was stopped by a patrol. There were the usual heavy-handed preliminaries: "Where are you going, citizen? Your papers!" Anyway, while I was fishing my papers out, one of the soldiers — just a boy, really, and wearing the flimsiest shoes you could imagine — bawled at me in a fearsome deep voice: "Where've you just come from?" So I told him: "From the hospital. I'm a doctor, going home from work." The boy-soldier said something to his mate, who made himself scarce, and then he whispered to me: "Could you fix me up with a gold tooth, pal?" Well, I was thrown by that. "A gold tooth?" I said. And then he poured his soul out to me: "It's something I've really set me heart on. I even dream about it at nights: goin' back to me village with all this gold sparklin' in me mouth. Go on, fix me up, be a pal!" So that's your iron revolutionaries for you! They've had a good look at all those gents they've stood against the wall, and now they've started dreaming of gold teeth. What a confounded shambles it's all turned into! And really, some of them you come across are little more than children.'

The conversation continued awkwardly, by fits and starts.

'Konstantin was the first to sense that it was time to go, and when he stood up, the other man followed suit. You may find this hard to believe, but I've no recollection of his face at all. I was just looking at Lydia and Nikolay Vasilyevich all the time. I can see them sitting there now, as clearly if it was yesterday: Lydia on a bench by the roaring stove, her head lowered, looking thin, wearing a black dress and with a grey shawl over her shoulders. Her face is pink, and her cheeks are glowing — that's from her high temperature, of course. Next to her is Nikolay Vasilyevich, his hair unkempt and almost completely grey, carefully lifting a cup of hot water to his lips. His eyes are red — he's terribly tired, hardly been sleeping at all. He talks slowly, all the time looking somewhere over the top of her head.'

Then, towards midnight (was Liza asleep? — she was, practically) a murmur of voices stirred in the next room.

'Thank you. Why don't you say anything, Kolya? Thank you...'

An angry whisper, breaking into a hoarse falsetto hiss, bit off the end of her timid phrase: 'Well, my dear, so that's what you have to say for yourself, is it? Thank you! What do you have to thank me for? Perhaps in future you'd at least be so good as to let me know whether to come home or stay the night at the hospital with all the typhoid cases! Perhaps one day you'll learn to think not just about yourself, but...'

'Please don't talk to me like that.' The transparent sibilance of her low muted voice came like a sudden shower of broken glass. 'You're being unfair now.'

'Unfair?'

Fully awake by now, her startled gaze fixed on the closed door, Liza could sense him clasping his head between his hands as he said this.

'Me, unfair? So why was it your lover didn't look after you all those times you were ill? Where was he, the footloose wanderer, when you were here with me, at death's door? Or was there too much of a risk he'd find you unattractive at times like that? He might have gone off you completely — who's interested in an invalid, after all? And to bring you that honey — how thoughtful, we can't even begin to express our gratitude! When will he be honouring us with another visit? Just be sure to let me know!'

Liza heard the patter of bare feet running across the floor, then a creaking sound as the wardrobe door was opened, and the hasty rustling of a dress being put on.

'I'm going, and don't try to stop me!'

'Where are you going?' he hissed. 'Where? Do you think anyone apart from me has the slightest interest in you?'

'Don't try to stop me!' Her voice broke into a scream. 'Let me out of here this instant! I can do without your charity! God almighty, I've just about had enough of everything!'

'Does that include our child? Such a devoted mother, our dear little Lydia! But then you'd had enough of us once before, do you remember?'

Suddenly everything went quiet on the other side of the closed door, and a minute later the sound of sobbing was heard. Unable to hold back any longer, Liza pushed the door slightly ajar. Nikolay Vasilyevich was sitting with his head in his hands on the blue bench next to the extinct stove, while Lydia stood half-dressed in the far doorway, a scarf thrown over her unbuttoned black dress, her hands hanging lifelessly at her sides. She was weeping uncontrollably, gasping for breath and coughing. Nikolay Vasilyevich stood up ponderously, reaching out towards but not touching her tear-stained, distorted face.

'Forgive me,' he said. 'In the name of God forgive me. Go back to bed, quickly now. You must stay in bed.'

Obediently she went to the sofa, undressed and slipped under the cherry-red quilt, her teeth chattering. She had begun to shiver feverishly.

'Liza!' called Nikolay Vasilyevich in his usual anxious voice. 'The stove, quickly! I have to sterilize the syringe, hurry now!'

'She became terribly weak after that night, although Nikolay Vasilyevich, who used to examine her chest every day, said her lungs were clearer. For some reason he put the weakness down to nerves and generally feeling run down after the long winter. Our main concern was to keep her from getting typhoid fever, which was cutting people down right, left and centre. The Potapovs — Yelena Sergeyevna and Dmitry Tikhonych — both went down with it at that time. Konstantin went to look after them, and Nikolay Vasilyevich forbade us to meet because of the danger of infection.'

In his delirium Potapov kept trying to get out of bed and

make off. Despite his advanced fever, this outwardly feeble old man had suddenly been endowed with a ferocious strength.

'Let me go, let me go!' he screamed, clawing Konstantin's hands off his body. 'Bastards! I'll escape anyway! I'll get out by sea! You can't drink the sea dry!'

By evening he had grown weary and calmed down, and his lined face with its growth of prickly stubble now wore an expression of childlike helplessness.

'Nothing, nothing,' he mumbled plaintively. 'I've nothing for you. You should have thought about it before, soldier lads — I've nothing for you now.'

As if attempting to hide, he pulled the rag soaked in vinegar that he had on his forehead down over his eyes, which he screwed up tight.

'I'm scared, I'm scared,' he gabbled. 'What are you threatening me like that for? Just you wait!' Then he burst into tears.

Towards the evening of the fifth day he suddenly regained lucidity and squeezed Konstantin's hand between his feeble fingers.

'Hello, Konstantin Andreyevich. These last few days I've been seeing you as if through rain on a window-pane. I kept thinking: is it you, or not? Sometimes it looked like you, but at other times it was like my old nanny with her knitting...'

He took a breath.

'Konstantin, bend down closer, it's hard for me to shout. That's better. Did I just imagine it, or is it true that the Bolsheviks have a special island somewhere on the Volga where they take anyone who's surplus to requirements? Someone may have told me about it, I don't remember. Old folk, little children, young ladies, invalids, limbless soldiers, starving peasants — anyone unlucky enough to incur their displeasure, in fact. They load them on a ferry at night and dump them on this island without food or water. Now you can snuff it, they say, and don't be too long about it. They don't waste bullets on them, just leave them to it... Can you hear me?'

'Dmitry Tikhonych, dear chap, you imagined it all.'

Potapov heaved a sigh.

'Konstantin, have you had no news at all from Stepan Obnovlensky?'

'No, how could I?'

'Get away from here, Konstantin. Things can only get worse. Save your seed: your children-to-be, your grandchildren and great-grandchildren. Take Liza with you, take your mother and sisters — get on a boat, and go!'

'It looks as if we've left it too late for that, Dmitry Tikhonych. Anyway, where would we go? You yourself have stayed here, haven't you?'

Potapov laid his hand with its tracery of swollen veins on Konstantin's. 'I have, that's true. You see, the way I reasoned, if your own country is a bad mother to you, how can you expect a foreign country to treat you any better as your stepmother? That may have been a useful analogy, or it may have been a stupid, tragic miscalculation on my part. I was partly swayed by my experience as a young man, too. I studied in Germany, you know, and I can remember to this day how homesick I felt there — homesick for my village, with its woodsmoke, its snow, its ramshackle little church... Oh, Konstantin, what a vast patchwork each one of us carries within him, all of it put there by God! And although we should dearly like to simplify His handiwork, it can't be done...' He licked his dry lips and closed his eyes. His face with its growth of prickly stubble still retained an expression of childlike helplessness.

When I go to Moscow, I shall buy a box of seedlings at the market — forget-me-nots — and plant them out on my grandfather's grave, covering the rough earth, that bad mother, with their scattering of blue...

I went away and left them. Now strangers come to tend their graves, locking the gate as they leave. I don't even have a key...

Why does this dream keep coming back to haunt me? I dream I've gone away and left her: left her as she was in those last weeks before she died, sitting lifelessly in the red armchair by the window, her dark, trembling fingers turning the crumbling pages of a prayer book. How could I go away and just leave her there like that?

Stop, don't be silly: it's only a dream! But why does it come back so often? At dead of night, while I am asleep here in this American city, she sits helpless in a red armchair by a window giving on to impenetrable Moscow rain, her dark, trembling fingers turning...

Forgive me, Lord. I went away, and left her there.

'How are you today, Lydia?'

'I slept all day — out like a light, I was. Then I opened my eyes and looked out of the window, and saw the sun shining, snow melting and dripping from the rooftops, sparrows hopping about... It was just like in childhood, those times when you'd be ill and have to stay in bed for a couple of weeks with a high fever

— and then all at once you'd fall into a deep sleep, and when you woke up you'd look through the window and see this fluffy cloud, and hear voices...'

'Yes,' said Liza with a sudden catch in her breath. 'And then Mummy would come in on tiptoe with a thermometer or a plate of raspberries...'

'My God,' cried Lydia, tears running down her cheeks. 'My God, I wonder how they're getting on there? Not even their letters get through. What a trial it all is!'

Each gazed into the other's tearful eyes that were so like her own.

'Liza!'

'What is it?'

'I'm going to die soon.'

'Don't talk such nonsense!'

'I just know. Daddy came to me in a dream yesterday. He was dressed in tails, as if he were going to the Assembly for the evening. His eyes were shining, and he said: "Come on, my dear, there's room for you in my carriage, let's go!" Of course, I knew he was dead, but somehow I couldn't say it, I felt awkward. So I whispered: "Just a minute, Daddy, what about Mummy?" And he answered in this calm, confident voice: "Go and tell Mummy that we'll be all right." Then I woke up.'

'Stop it!' said Liza without turning round, as she furiously fanned the damp firewood packed into the stove. 'Stop it, I don't even want to hear!'

'I remember how much I missed Konstantin for those three weeks when he was looking after the Potapovs, and how angry I felt towards Nikolay Vasilyevich for forbidding us to see each other. I was even angry with Lydia for not understanding how I felt. But I couldn't disobey Nikolay Vasilyevich. Konstantin sent me notes every day. He missed me terribly, too, and felt lost without me.'

She woke up, her heart pounding. It was just growing light. 'What's today?' she thought. 'The ninth of March... Surely by the end of this week I'll be able to see him again — how much longer can it drag on?' Who was that woman with the dark eyes she'd seen in her dream? A gypsy? God, what nonsense one dreamt at times!

'Liza-a!'

Why did Nikolay Vasilyevich's voice sound so strange?

'Liza-a!'

She rushed into the adjoining room. There, deathly pale in the freezing, flickering half-light, his grey hair fanning up from his forehead, stood Nikolay Vasilyevich: horror-struck, pointing with outspread fingers towards the cherry-red quilt. Lydia lay peacefully beneath the quilt, her eyebrows sharply raised, her auburn plait draped across the pillow, one cheek resting on cupped hands. A thin trickle of saliva glistened on her chin.

'Can't you see?' said Nikolay Vasilyevich almost inaudibly, his whole body shaking. 'She's... dead...'

The station was packed to bursting with gaunt figures in puttees carrying sacks, women cradling grey underfed babies in their arms, youths with caps pulled down over their eyes, malicious-eyed peasant women wearing shawls wrapped crosswise over the chest. A bluish-grey haze of cheap tobacco smoke hung in the sunny spring air.

'They'll be announcing your train any minute,' he said, on edge, pressing her tightly to him. 'Darling, I just hope you manage to make it there in all this bedlam! God knows I'm concerned enough about letting you go, I really am!'

'Don't worry, I'll get there all right.' She was not crying, but her eyes as they lingered on his face were still red from recent tears. 'Only please, please come yourself as soon as you can!'

'Don't worry about Koko,' he whispered hurriedly, showering her hair, hands and cheeks with kisses. 'I'll make sure to visit them regularly, and Nikolay Vasilyevich too. And as soon as circumstances permit, I'll join you. I love you more than life itself.'

The train made slow progress, stopping frequently. She found herself now sinking into a heavy sleep, now with searing clarity returning to the real world around her.

There had been a light fall of snow on the morning of the funeral: glistening snowflakes that flew swiftly down from a bright sky far above, to lie without melting on Lydia's face.

Merciful God, was it really true? She could feel the sharp rhythmic jolting of the wheel axles working its way painfully into her body from beneath the carriage floor. She adjusted her holdall, which kept slipping from under her head, and closed her eyes firmly.

Lydia was dead. She'd gone. There was just an empty space now under the cherry-red quilt.... How peaceful her face had been...

What shall I say to Mummy, she thought, how am I going to break it to her? Lord, what have we done to deserve Thy punishment?

Nikolay Vasilyevich had taken Koko to the open coffin. 'He's eleven years old,' he'd said. 'Let him say goodbye to his mother.' Koko had looked at his mother from under his fair eyelashes. *How* he had looked at her!

Unable to tear himself away, his hands trembling, Nikolay Vasilyevich had stood there, straightening her hair. Her auburn tresses, gold at the temples.

She couldn't bear to think of it.

Four months ago she had been sent by her mother to Moscow to help Lydia; now, having buried Lydia, she was returning to her mother in Tambov. Lord, what have we done to deserve...

It was cold in the basement of their former house in what had once been Dvoryanskaya Street. There were five of them seated round the table, which had a clean white cloth on it: Liza and Sasha, their mother, their grandmother, and Nanny. Liza tried not to look at her father's bed with its white bedspread. Her mother was weeping quietly. The terrible news had been broken some days before.

'Why don't you go and see Musya?' Nanny said in a low voice. 'You can see that awful man she's got engaged to.'

'What awful man?'

'That fiance, she's landed herself with. Round-eyed fellow with big ears — a Bolshevik, he is. I really don't know what she sees in him.'

It turned out that Musya was engaged to Misha Pavlenkov, who in his time had been thrown out of secondary school for unsatisfactory progress. Liza had seen him at the skating rink sometimes, many years ago. Now it was with some surprise that she looked at him. He was thin, really did have big ears, and spoke in crackling bursts of slogan-like phrases. He was adamant about not getting married in church: 'a), I'm a Communist, and b), an atheist. No need to elaborate on that, I hope.'

One day she did actually ask Musya, 'Can you honestly say you love him?'

Musya flushed deep red. 'Liza,' she said, 'he comes from such a desperately poor, disadvantaged family. His father drank, and his mother was in bad health all her life. Seven children, there were. He told me himself how he used to black in the holes in his shoes with ink. And then all of a sudden came the Revolution. It changed everything completely, and he put his faith in it right from the beginning. Of course, things are hard now for people like you and me, or your Sasha, for instance. But that's because we lived a charmed life before. We had things easy then, but for people like him it was hard going, and that wasn't fair, was it?'

'But you yourself said his father drank. What if my father, God forbid, had drunk or played cards from morning till night — do you think we'd have had an easy life?'

Musya put her hands over her ears, and her light-blue eyes filled with tears.

'You're wrong, Liza! You're overlooking the whole scale of the process now under way. The Revolution has brought the people happiness. The people...'

'Do you call *this* happiness?'

She gestured with her reddish-brown muff at the grimy, crumpled-looking street, which was empty apart from the odd hunched passer-by. Musya wiped her eyes with the palms of her hands.

'That's what he says. I don't know...'

There was a stench of death in the air. She had noticed it as soon as she got off the train and took her first steps through the streets of her home town.

The black park benches in the central public gardens had sunk quite some way into the ground. Hunched shadowy figures, their eyes lowered, trampled the dry snow as they hastened past. The news was all depressing. The Governor's daughter, Tanya Babanina, a beautiful girl with green eyes, had first tried unsuccessfully to kill herself and then run away, nobody knew where to. Tanya Subbotina had had twins, a boy and a girl, who had died after surviving for less than two months. Lily Golovkina had got a job as a typist in an office. On her application form, in answer to the question on social background, she had written: 'Father: road-sweeper.'

'Fancy slandering the dead like that,' Nanny sighed. 'What a man he was! A pillar of society, and a real gentleman. He and your father used to sit in the drawing-room, smoking their cigars... Road-sweeper, indeed!'

'I'd given up hoping for anything. I'd even given up hoping for Konstantin to arrive. No letters were getting through, the same as before. There was no food to be had anywhere. Nanny ground up grains of rye to make kasha, and acorn coffee was an unheard-of luxury. Sasha was unwell, and he was always complaining of hunger. He'd spend hour after hour just walking around the basement with his eyes shut, mumbling poems by Blok. Sometimes I thought he was going mad. At the beginning of May all the nettles disappeared from the streets and courtyards. People had taken them for soup.'

Close to where I am sitting here in Boston a young mother and her two curly-headed children have installed themselves for a picnic lunch on the grass. There is an appetizing smell of sandwiches and popcorn. It is summer now in Moscow, too.

In memory I conjure up the dusty, sultry heat of Moscow, its streets, its queues, the stifling crush of food stores with puddles of spilt milk on the floor and the smell of heated human bodies. I conjure up the Zagorsk train carrying me to our dacha, with string bags slung over shoulders, clutched in hands or swaying from hooks by the windows. My ice cream is melting in its wafer cup and dripping down on my skirt. I lean forward to wipe it off with my elbow, as my hand is taken up with a heavy bag.

A quite young, dark-skinned woman of haggard appearance is walking through the carriages, begging for money. With her left hand she clutches a pale, dark-eyed child, dressed in spite of the heat in a woollen hat, while her right hand is held extended in front of her. Some give, others do not. The heat in Moscow is unbearable. The whole green summer expanse of the city, a-flutter with birds, oozes irritation and fatigue.

Now, sitting here on the grass with pencil in hand, I feel ashamed. The memory of that weary, poverty-stricken child in the sweat-soaked woollen hat, gazing at my melting ice cream with such a sad expression in his dark eyes, fills me with a deep and burning sense of shame. The pungent smell of half-eaten sandwiches, mingled with water-melon freshness from the short grass, jars on my senses.

Don't judge me too harshly, soul... My nomadic soul, show forbearance...

'I was working for the same government agency as Lala —

I'd taught myself to type, which didn't take much doing. We were paid in rations. Sasha had gone into a decline, and Grandma had rheumatism so badly she could hardly walk. Living in that damp basement didn't help much, either. I just seemed to be stuck in a groove, living mechanically, glad to get through each day. And then one day, towards evening...'

And then one day, towards evening, a young, very thin woman in an old dark-blue dress was perching on a grimy narrow window-sill in the stairwell, trying clumsily to light the straggling cigarette she had rolled herself, when the door to the street flew open, and, looking straight into her dark eyes — which stared back as if paralysed from beneath her lynx-tuft eyelashes — a tall man carrying a battered leather portmanteau came bounding up the stairs towards her.

'The rest you know, Anya. A week later we were married, and eighteen months after that Tomka was born.'

The beach at Lynn, with its smell of rotting seaweed and tame wide-eyed seagulls, is nearly empty. I walk over wet sands lacquered smooth by the water. Soon the tide will be coming in to lick away my footsteps. How did I come to be here? Quite simply, by driving half an hour from Boston. But seriously: what chance wind brought me...

A Russian boy, his fists clenched with the effort, singing a romance to words by Sasha Chorny.

Ah, what trivial detail, what chance encounter can sometimes be enough to...

Yes, she went away, to Paris, and then for a long time slept, shrouded again and again by stinging Moscow snows, to wake up now, here in Lynn.

Greetings, dear soul! Do you recognize me? Are you glad we've met? And do you remember that poem of Alexander's, written not long before he and Liza picked water-lilies at Chudin Pond? Surely you do?

> *With swelling voice exultantly she sings*
> *And onwards through ethereal regions wings —*
> *Through icy realms we all one day must know:*
> *My dearest, long since freed from life and care,*
> *All love, all tears now spent, her plaited hair*
> *Still tied with ribbon in a crumpled bow...*

*Lala,*

*Natasha,*

*Toma*

*I* came across this photograph almost by chance. When we went through customs, in fact, what worried me most was that the customs officer — that one with the blond hair and the moustache — wouldn't let me take any photographs out of the country. Leaving people behind, I'd taken their faces with me; leaving graves, I'd taken the living, caught in frozen, faded images: on the porch with a dog; surrounded by bottles at a name-day party; wearing a straw hat at an angle underneath a beach awning; holding children in their arms or on their knees.

Little Grandma with her reassuring eyes was tucked away in my pocket. Yet the blond customs officer even let my photo album through. Using for some reason the point of his penknife, he pulled out a snapshot of me as a child: a skinny girl with protruding ribs, sitting on a massive rock by the sea at Koktebel. My head — in profile, with a ribbon tied in a bow — is turned towards the sky, and "Me, dreaming of happiness" is scrawled across the waves in indelible pencil. Something prompted him to examine this photograph suspiciously for a quite unnecessary length of time. Eventually he replaced it neatly, and a look of bravado sneaked across his face as he snapped the album shut. So I managed to get the whole lot out, the whole glossy pile, including this snapshot. My goodness, it's faded... Even so I can tell it was taken on the veranda of our dacha before it was glassed in, years ago, before I was even born — although I still remember that couch that looks like a dachshund. I don't remember the wickerwork table, though — it must have been thrown out or given away after this was taken. And there they are, the three of them, sitting on the veranda, which was still open then: my mother and Lala on the couch and Natasha at the wickerwork table. They have garlands of camomile in their hair. My mother has her right arm round Lala's shoulders, and her left hand is resting on the head of a cat, asleep on her lap (I know they used to have a pink cat called Rosa before I was born). My mother has a sad expression on her face, as she always does in all her photographs. I was so young when she died, it's as if she's doing it deliberately, just to let me know how sad she always was. There she sits in that frozen posture with her right hand on Lala's shoulder and her left on the cat's pink fur, a garland of camomile in her hair. There's a lilac tree on one side, its dark foliage trailing right down on to the couch, Lala's shoulders, my mother's arm and the cat's head. I wasn't even born then.

It was just after the war. They were students, and still the same good friends they had been since childhood days, although they were all at different colleges. Now I know that life shuffles all the cards, that princes can marry paupers, and so on, and that's all very fine. But it just so happened that these three girls were all offspring of the former nobility, and their thin-skinned cold lives were imbued with an intuitive sense of danger. They knew for instance why Toma's mother had stayed up all night scraping the gilt inscription "For Faith in Tsar and Fatherland" off their delicate blue china after Olga's husband was arrested (red-haired, blue-eyed Olga, so pretty that everyone called her "Poppet"). They knew why Natasha's father drank and spent most of his time at the races; why, strumming gypsy romances on a guitar, he would say to his wife (herself a gypsy, whom he had once, in better times, persuaded to elope with him from her gypsy clan): 'What are you so angry about, my dear? I live as my grandfathers lived before me; as for them, they can...' (at which point he would make an expressive and rather indecent gesture). To this she would respond in silence, merely wrapping herself more tightly in her frayed shawl and inhaling slowly on her long cigarette.

As for Lala, who lived in a basement with her mother, sister and two maiden aunts, she was embarrassed by a quite unnecessary number of things in life: her French surname; her pronunciation of the letter 'r' (also French); her aunt's pince-nez; their poverty; the Easter festivities which her mother celebrated despite their poverty with old-world lavishness, presenting their friends with intricately decorated eggs and napkins embroidered with doves and forget-me-nots. They also knew yet another, quite special fear, sometimes expressed in the scarcely utterable letters 'NKVD': a grey, oppressive, immovable fear, like that grey, oppressive building on the Lubyanka with its statue of the wiry figure with the pointed beard in his long greatcoat.

Only to Natasha and Toma could Lala mention that her father never referred to Lenin other than as 'that syphilitic'. She told them this in an embarrassed whisper as the three of them were walking to their homes in snowbound Neopalimovsky Lane and in First Workers' Street — walking quickly, chilled to the bone as they were in their flimsy shoes and knitted head-scarves. They were nearly seventeen; it was towards the end of their last winter at school, the winter of 1940, and they had just endured a long and gruelling wait in the queue for the Lenin mausoleum where he lay behind glass in his coffin: wrinkled, yellow, parchment-like. The syphilitic.

But on that golden-green July day they wandered on and on through the forest, swam in the creamy black waters of a forest lake with lots of water lilies, and then suddenly came upon a whole field of camomile. They gathered three enormous armfuls of the flowers and made garlands of them for their hair. When they arrived back at the dacha, one of the neighbours was there, a lanky middle-aged fellow who for a long time had been foolishly and hopelessly smitten with Toma. There and then he took a photo of them on the veranda, which was still open in those days. Then Natasha, whose gypsy blood sometimes stirred within her, looked at the heavy, golden-eyed camomile flowers and exclaimed: 'What are we going to do with all these flowers? Let's go and sell them!'

Toma seconded the idea with enthusiasm, and Lala, blushing as usual, also agreed. Standing on a patch of ground next to the station, they sold the flowers off much faster than expected, and only Lala still had three bunches left when they were approached by a bulky, broad-shouldered man in an unbuttoned white shirt. Supporting himself on crutches, he stopped in front of them, his eyes lingering on Natasha. With her wide-set eyes and black eyebrows she had always taken first prize for looks, whether at school, in the street or at the Music Academy. Then his gaze shifted to the curly-headed Lala, who blushed furiously.

'How much are the flowers?' he asked, his half-closed velvety eyes seeming to caress her.

Aware of the hot blood flushing her chest, back and shoulders, and seeing with her lowered eyes no more than the sewn-up bottom of his trouser leg, she replied in a voice suddenly hoarse and strange, 'A rouble.'

'All right, give me two, then we'll all be happy,' he said in a deep resonant voice. 'Otherwise you'll be stuck here, and we won't be able to go for a walk.'

The other two went back to the dacha on their own, leaving her with the one-legged stranger. He gave them a mock-reassuring wave as, walking away, they turned to look back in surprise while she stayed behind.

In the jolting suburban train they let the warm evening breeze blow through their hair. The train clattered to a halt at dimly lit wooden platforms. There was a scent of jasmine, cicadas chirruped away in the night, and they held their faces up to the breeze whistling in through the carriage window, unaware as yet that this was it, the beginning.

The granite bench was still wet from a recent shower. They sat down, and he at once put his right arm round her and squeezed so hard she was afraid his fingers would leave red marks on her skin. However, she said nothing, and he squeezed her slender shoulder harder and harder, turning her face towards him with the palm of his free left hand and studying it at leisure as one might some colourful picture in a magazine.

'So, your name's Lala? Is that short for Olga or Yelena? And how come your surname's French — did you come to Moscow with Napoleon? Come on, tell me, don't be shy.'

Well aware that he was not really interested in anything she had to say, she all the same whispered a few incoherent words in explanation of her French surname; but before she could finish, a shock went through her body as she felt his hand touch her breast inside her unbuttoned woollen cardigan.

\* \* \*

'She's out of her mind, you know — completely obsessed with him, can't leave him alone! She goes to meet him at his works entrance, every evening — never misses! Not to mention keeping him in food, which she smuggles out of the house at every opportunity. Irina Avgustovna sees what's going on but doesn't say anything. Nor does Musya, nor Polina and Jeanette. They just keep quiet the whole time, the lot of them. Or else cry. I rang her yesterday just before midnight, but she wasn't in. I don't think she spent the night at home, I think she was with him. It's just a feeling I've got. Don't you have anything to say, Toma?'

'Yes, I do. I know she didn't spend the night at home, because she came to our house at three o'clock in the morning, on foot from Shabolovka Street. He'd thrown her out.'

'Wha-at?'

'That's right — thrown her out, just like that, for heaven's sake. He was drunk, and in a vile temper. Said he'd no use for her any more. She was crying her eyes out like... well, I can't even describe it, it was just a nightmare. She burst in on us in the middle of the night, her face all red and puffed-up from crying, and said he'd thrown her out but she couldn't live without him. Mummy said: "He's just an animal, a drunken animal! What did you ever see in him?" But she stood her ground like Joan of Arc: "I won't hear you say such things! You mustn't talk like that!"

You remember that time in the summer when she drank all the tea in the samovar on her own for a bet? Nearly burst, she did! And it's the same now: she'll go under first rather than listen to anyone else.'

'You think he won't marry her, then?'

'On the contrary, I think he will. Where else would he find a sucker like her?'

His heavy crutches with iron rivets lay sprawled on the floor next to the bed. She moved fitfully about the room, followed by the heavy gaze of his hazel eyes, watching her as she picked up scattered clothes, flicked away dust, poured hot water into the washing-up bowl.

'Feed the canary,' he said lethargically, and lit a cigarette.

'The canary? Yes, of course!'

She started making twittering, cooing noises next to the round iron cage in which the little red-eyed canary was singing away with all the power its tiny yellow throat could muster.

'Sounds like you at night. Except I don't think he's got quite as much to sing about, eh?' he smirked, waving the smoke away with the back of his hand.

She kneeled down by the bed and pressed her face, framed by little fair curls, into the pillow, breathing in the familiar scents of his hair, his cigarettes, his skin... His lazy, hot hand with its nicotine-yellow fingers pinched her ear, then slipped into the open neck of her nightdress. She lifted her flushed face.

'Mummy would like us to get married in church...'

...Stop, I tell myself, this is all my imagination, nothing

more... Was there a canary? Was there a wedding? Like a bather, slowly and hesitantly entering the water and pushing it from him with the palms of his hands, I too push away the foam of details frothing before me: a church at the intersection of two roads, one evening in autumn; the bride in a dress run up from a tulle curtain; the bridegroom, slightly tipsy, with medal ribbons on his chest; an aunt wearing a purple scarf, her pince-nez bedewed with tears — all this I push away. I am tired. The page is white beneath my hands.

...Stop, I tell myself. What actually happened? What do I remember?

As always, snow, which plays the leading role in all my memories: I am walking along Devichka Avenue, which is swathed in white to its linden eyebrows. Leo Tolstoy stands pastel-pink and frowning in the middle of the street, his enormous stone hands held behind his back, while an ageing woman dressed in a shabby fur coat comes hobbling towards me. Since my mother died I have seen her four times or so, no more, and now I am shocked at how she has aged. I can't just call her Lala, but I don't think I can remember her patronymic. Would Yelena be in order? As she draws level, she lets out a gasp of recognition, clasps me to her bosom with her grey darned mittens, from inside one of which comes a jingling sound (of keys, or coins?), and, burying her face in my collar, starts to cry.

'Mummy had this strange dream last night,' said Natasha, her eyebrows raised in wonderment. 'They're all mad keen on dreams in our house, you know,' she continued, lowering her voice. 'My father keeps having the same dream over and over again: he's flogging a horse to death, and then he buries it all by himself at night somewhere on the edge of a deserted village. Anyway, that's by the way — this is what Mummy told us: "I dreamt there was a snake living in our bookcase: a small black snake with big eyes that were somehow malicious and yet almost human. And it was living right there amongst the books, between Aksakov and the encyclopedia..." '

Toma burst out laughing. Logs crackled in the stove, turning from flickering red to ash-grey and black as they burned down. They were sitting on the sofa, nibbling pretzels. The cat lay curled up in a ball, fast asleep.

'No, wait, don't laugh. I laughed too at first, but now I can't get the stupid thing out of my head. So anyway, there's this snake living here, and for some reason we don't feed it. I don't know why, when you think my father would feed sugar to the mice in the kitchen if you let him. Anyway, we don't feed the snake, and we can see it wasting away in front of us. And then suddenly Mummy asks me to give it some milk. And apparently we're all horrified that up to then none of us had even thought of giving the snake some milk, to feed the poor creature up a bit. And Mummy hands me the milk and says: "Put it there, on that book, and then get out of the way fast." I go up to the snake with the milk, and Mummy and I can see it lying there barely alive, squashed beneath the books, with its eyes shut. But as soon as I put the saucer down in front of it, it uncoils and goes for me with its poisonous tongue. Right in the face!'

'My God, what a horror story!' Toma started laughing again. 'What happened then?'

'It's all very well poking fun...' began Natasha, but then

laughed herself, as if retelling the dream had helped her exorcize her own fear. 'That was all. Mummy woke up in tears and hasn't been herself all day. "Believe me, it's a bad omen," she keeps saying.'

Her trouble was that she was too good-looking. Being beautiful doesn't make a person good, I remember being told as a child. Yet all the things I heard about her seemed to confirm that she was good as well as beautiful. 'A real-life Anna Karenina!' my grandma would sometimes add. He on the other hand was unprepossessing, or at least very ordinary in appearance. And it just so happened that she loved him, but he didn't love her. Other men would have gladly blown their brains out or hanged themselves on her account, would have grovelled on their knees for her; but she didn't want any of them, only this one who, far from blowing his brains out or grovelling, simply treated her like dirt. She was often in tears, and then all those who loved her would cry too and appeal to her: 'Why don't you leave him? Are you out of your mind, or what?' But she would always reply: 'No, I'll never do that.'

Such was the picture that formed in my six-year-old mind; and that was how I drew her in coloured pencils on the coarse-textured paper of my drawing book: wearing an enormously wide skirt and with golden hair down to her ankles, her arms stretched out towards a man with a long nose and big moustache in a frock coat from the time of Pushkin. To one side of them a tree with green leaves, and above them a sun with rays fanning out. Nothing else. The picture of a life; the picture of a love. People invariably called the beautiful lady in my drawing book Natasha, although the real Natasha had black hair, and in any case I had hardly ever seen her. But whenever grandma talked to me about her, she would always add: 'My God, that poor woman! And so beautiful, too! So beautiful.'

The young man with the expensive deerskin hat and the slight scar above his upper lip impatiently flicked snow from the base of Chaikovsky's statue with his glove. Warily alert, as if poised to take off from his marble elevation, Chaikovsky spun melodies audible to himself alone around fingers held up in a feminine pose, paying no attention to the fussy sparrow that was hopping up and down on his frozen head.

'Please don't tell me I'm late again, Vitaly?'

He turned abruptly at the sound of her anxious voice. A white head-scarf glistening with snow; snow glistening on black hair; high-set eyebrows, wet eyelashes — yes, she really was beautiful. And as poor as one of Dostoyevsky's heroines. He'd read a couple of those novels, and had found them pretty slushy. But this family from Neopalimovsky Lane would have suited the famous epileptic down to the ground. Colourful wasn't the word for them! Ma was good for a laugh in her tattered shawl, and pa was pretty good, too: a real upper-class toff with a plum in his mouth, a connoisseur of horse and hound who should have been out hunting hares on his heavily mortgaged estate instead of sitting by the stove knocking back vodka. Their rings and bracelets had long since gone to the pawnbroker's, their Baccarat crystal was all smashed. Talk about living relics! How had they all managed to survive? Just look at how they refused to lie down, how they still gave themselves airs! — 'Pray tell me, young man, where did you

make my daughter's acquaintance?' What a farce! He'd felt like
telling him: 'I made your daughter's acquaintance on a tram, mate,
and now she and I are going to... you know what.' Well, no, to be
honest — that could wait a bit until she'd got to know him better.
She had gypsy blood in her, the little dark beauty. Yes, that could
wait a bit — it would be all the better for it. But he was going to
sleep with the old man's daughter, and the old man had better
believe it. It was all his, all this snow-clad, black-browed beauty.
Until he got fed up with her, that was. Then he'd take it from
there.

And with a laugh he squeezed the warm hand she held out
to him and said: 'For you, Natasha, I could wait a lifetime.'

Her father kept topping up his glass from the little blue
decanter. He held his little finger extended, and the long manicured
nail trembled slightly. She listened to her parents' conversation
from the semi-darkness of her small room, where she was practising
her scales. It was more of a monologue than a conversation, for as
usual her mother merely threw in a guttural: 'O-oh!' on the rare
occasions when her father paused in his flow.

'What do we know about him? What's your view of him, my
dear? A nasty little upstart on the make, that's what I think. One
of *their* lot. I've got a nose for that sort.' He sniffed noisily. 'Spawn
of the devil, he is. But small fry, not one of your first-rank demons.
What do you think, my dear? As for the way he looks at her,' he
continued with a clink of the blue decanter, 'I find that disgusting.
Dis-gusting! Undresses her with his eyes in my presence! Can
you remember me ever looking at you that way? I didn't even
dare touch your plait! But as for this lot... Disgusting. All right,

we used to go to a brothel — not when we were at school, mind, this was much, much later. Even so, we didn't know where to look: we had a conscience, you see, a sense of shame. Burning shame. But nothing bothers this lot. Gangsters, they are. What do you think, my dear? I've started having terrible nightmares again. A few nights ago I dreamt he was chewing her fingers off. She was playing the piano, practising for a concert, and he went up to her and bent over her hands as if to kiss them. And suddenly I could see blood...'

A deep guttural: 'O-oh!' was wrenched from her mother's throat.

'He took her to Germany with him,' my grandma told me later. 'She was already pregnant. He married her because someone in his position was expected to have a wife. Your grandfather and I always thought he worked for the NKVD. To start with she said he was in the armed forces and that he was being sent to Germany for a tour of duty. We never saw him in military uniform, only ever in civilian clothes. And always well-dressed and clean-shaven: always smartly turned out. She came to see your mother and told her she was expecting. She was afraid of him, afraid of going abroad with him, and afraid of having the baby. So beautiful, she was! She went anyway.'

\* \* \*

It has been a dull, rainy spring this year. I sit hammering the keys of my typewriter. I too have been having dreams, and am prey to so many anxieties. Yesterday I went to the hospital to visit an eight-year-old little girl. 'Do come, she wants to see you,' her mother had said on the phone. The girl has a brain tumour, and the results of the biopsy will be made known tomorrow. I dial the hospital and hear a child's voice: 'Come again. Surprise me.' I am choked by tears. Yes, so many anxieties...

\* \* \*

So, she came to see my mother. She banged on the torn felt of the door with her fist (there was no bell), and my mother let her in.

'I got frozen through coming here, Toma,' she said. 'Some weather for March! Could I have something hot to drink? Tea, or just hot water'll be fine.'

It was mild outside. The snow was thawing, icicles were melting. Winter was dying for all to see. Dissolving in tears, clinging on to collars and scarves with its last tiny barbs, it was saying farewell. Yet nobody showed the slightest concern.

'How could you get cold? It's really mild, I've opened all the top windows. Come into the kitchen, and we'll put the kettle on.'

In the kitchen, with its painted wooden floor and rubber plant sponged glistening-clean on the windowsill, an ancient crone was shuffling about in slippers. This was Matryona, who lived just across the hall from the toilet in a dark, poky little room plastered with icon prints and packed full of trunks. In bad weather she would lie dozing on a pile of rags on one of the trunks; whenever it was fine she was out begging in Vagankov Cemetery. Now she sctrutinized them critically from beneath her shaggy grey eyebrows.

'Bless my soul if it ain't pretty little Natasha!' she exclaimed. 'But how come you've gone all yeller like that?'

My mother was about to cut off some of their rationed grey bread, but Natasha stayed her hand.

'I'm not hungry, Toma,' she said. 'Don't give me anything, I'll just have tea. I can't eat, I feel sick all the time.'

Then she told her everything. Clearly I can hear her telling my mother about everything, including the baby. And my mother whispered, 'Leave him. Are you out of your mind, or what?'

'How can I leave him? I can't live without him. But you have to understand, it's not love — no, I don't love him. Every day I think to myself: I won't go to the phone — but then like an idiot I do. I don't want to see him, but go running all the same. My God!

'=Anyway, it's too late now. He's being sent to work in Germany, and I'm going with him. I'll have the baby there. In any case, there's no shame in having it after six months instead of nine, is there? We're not having a wedding reception: I don't want one, and nor does he. It'll just be him and me, my parents and you. And then off to Germany straight afterwards. If only you knew how scared I am of him! I feel so terribly awkward, too, when he undresses me, and when he looks me over like that. He's had lots of women, I know.'

'Did he tell you?'

'Yes, and he found it quite amusing, too. He said, "That's funny: all women are white in the dark, but you're brown." '

Then my mother started to cry. Her tears sprang not from pity or fear for Natasha, but from the unbearable tension which had first caused Natasha's face to flush bright red and her eyebrows to snap and droop from the middle, before flooding across into her as well. She cried, while Natasha sat motionless, her eyebrows drooping, her fingers tightly clenched. Then Natasha whispered, 'Just a minute, I feel sick,' and rushed out of the room. My mother rushed after her and then stood still outside the toilet, where she could hear her choking and crying: 'O-oh!' in a low guttural voice just like her gypsy mother.

Unheard-of riches were laid out on the yellowed tablecloth: opalescent pink salmon, black caviar, cheese with neat elongated holes, white bread that melted in the mouth. Natasha's father, as always, kept on topping up his glass from the little blue decanter. The bridegroom seemed somewhat irritated and was eating greedily, as if eager to assert seigneurial rights over all these delicacies supplied by him. Natasha's mother snuggled into her shawl, her dark fingers braiding and unbraiding the end of her plait, which she had not pinned up.

'Might I make so bold as to enquire, Vitaly,' her father said, his manicured little finger fluttering uncontrollably, 'where delicacies such as these are to be had? In what underground palaces are they kept hidden away?'

The bridegroom was chewing on a piece of salmon and did not respond immediately. 'Why, what's it to you?' he said.

'To me? Why, nothing at all, of course not. Idle curiosity. And don't you worry, my dear,' he added, catching the familiar glance thrown in his direction. 'I was just asking an innocent question — quite innocent — as what you might call a close relative. Just wanted to raise one of the curtains of secrecy for a brief instant.'

'Better leave those curtains alone,' said the bridegroom, loosening his tie with a sharp jerk of the head. 'People have worked and fought, risking their lives, and now they're enjoying their just rewards. While they're still alive, that is. They're all flesh and blood like anyone else, you know.'

'Ah, so that's it!' There was a clink of the blue decanter. The dark fingers started braiding the plait even faster. 'Risking their lives, enjoying their just rewards? Well, do you know what, I can't bear to walk down the street. I can't bear the sight of all those limbless cripples — all those, as you might say, glorious heroes: airmen, sailors, tank-men, with their wooden legs now and begging for alms. And it's not everyone that gives them something. In fact, let's be honest, not many do: people are too impoverished. Even more so in spirit. It's quite appalling, the way they live now. And I include both aspects in that, what's more: the practical and the spiritual, as you might say, I...'

'What are you blethering on about? All this "I, I, I!" It's easy enough for you to talk, sitting by the stove drinking your vodka! Limbless cripples... There'll be special homes for invalids built, they'll have a decent enough life. Can't all be done at once. But to go around with a hostile attitude, sniffing out shortcomings — that, let me tell you, is the lowest thing anyone can stoop to! And if you take my advice you'll stop it before you live to regret it!'

'My dear fellow, what can you be hinting at?' There was another clink of the blue decanter. 'The Lubyanka? But I'm practically immune to fear by now. Nearly thirty years I've been shaking in my shoes — how long can one keep that up? Or will you be going to report me straight after the wedding celebration? Don't let me stop you. And there's no need for you to turn pale, my dear — what can he do to me? He can hardly think of anything worse than what he's done already.'

The bridegroom stood up. He seemed to Toma to be assessing the situation. Apart from himself there were four persons seated round the yellowed tablecloth. It was essentially a safe enough situation. Apart from which...

'Well, that's it: party's over. I'll come for you by car just before the train leaves. And make sure you're ready: the driver can't wait. As for you, my dear relations, I must leave you now with a heavy heart...'

Throwing his light-coloured raincoat over his arm, he left, slamming the door behind him. Nobody said a word. And then, abandoning her plait, Natasha's mother stood up, went across to where Natasha sat motionless and deathly white and, covering her daughter's head with her shawl, clasped it to her stomach...

'...Now this one,' said grandma, taking a large photograph out of its rice-paper wrapping, 'this one she sent from Germany. Come on, drink up your milk, otherwise your throat'll never get better! Drink it while it's hot, and be glad you can stay off school. Look, that's Natasha with her daughter. She was six months old then. Anya — Natasha named her after her mother.'

One had gone away and had a baby daughter. The other was near enough, but meetings with her had become an ordeal. She only ever dropped in for a brief stay, always looking scared and with red blotches on her round face. She would kiss them all in turn (Toma, Toma's mother, the cat) and then start crying. What was most distressing was that she never told them anything. Or rather, what she did say gave the appearance of everything being just fine. Did he drink? Yes, a bit. Less than he used to. Was his heart still giving him trouble? No, not any more: Jeanette had cured him with herbal remedies. Did he love her? Here her round face would take on a condescending expression. Yes, he loved her very much, but what man would admit to that, especially one who'd been through the war? Just a week ago their canary had died — suffocated, as canaries sometimes do — and he'd cried. He'd sat there, drinking and crying. Then, when the bottle was empty, he'd said: 'Go and chuck the canary in the rubbish bin.'

'So what did you do?'

'What did I do? I said: "Kolya, perhaps we could bury it?" '

'And what did he say?'

'Nothing, he just waved me away.'

'So what are you crying for?'

'Me, crying? I'm just telling you what happened...'

Toma was upset, and wanted to help as well, but at the time she herself was inexcusably happy. It is a sad fact that our happiness never coincides with that of those we love. Happiness is something we experience alone, just as we do unhappiness.

What was I doing that day when Tanya was stung by a wasp, and the sting proved fatal?

\* \* \*

That small intensive-care ward, blind rain on the window and, lying enmeshed in wires and tubes, my Tanya: in a coma, unmoving, eyes closed, already cast off from this life and not yet moored in the next, calm and impassive, testing with her bare foot the cold waters of that invisible river, gesturing to the unconcerned boatman with her exposed arm, herself dull white on the white sands of frozen time; my Tanya, completely alone.

And even if I had been there on the other shore, there is nothing I could have done to change things, to hold her back, to save her...

* * *

'They're so happy together. Don't you know what it means to be in love?' said my grandma sweetly to the red-cheeked policeman who was gazing at her with a vacant look.

The policeman turned even brighter red and cupped his hands together on his knees. It was morning, and their conversation was taking place in front of the evergreen rubber plant, which had been sponged glistening-clean. They sat facing one another on stools: my grandma, keen-eyed and graceful, and the nice young police officer who had called to ascertain by what authority a certain tenant with an unpronounceable name was domiciled at flat 4, No.4, First Workers' Street. Shtapinets, was it? Shtanimets? Shtanets?

'Yes,' said my grandma, smiling brightly, and for the first time finding a representative of the dreaded powers-that-be not as dread as they usually were. 'You're absolutely right, it's impossible to pronounce. Only if you break it down into syllables: Shtah-een-mets.'

'Strike a light,' the policeman groaned. 'Shtan... Come again?'

'Not Shtan,' grandma corrected him gently, 'but Shtayn, then a pause, and then — mets: Shtayn-mets! Now you try it!'

'Shtam...' the policeman ventured, '-yets!'

'Nearly, nearly,' grandma reassured him. 'And anyway, it's not important, is it? So do you agree with me? They're in love, you see, and want to be together. What else can they do?'

'Why we've had to bother you,' the policeman confided in a deep voice, 'is because of a certain irregularity as has come to our notice. They're living together, no doubt about that, but with different addresses on their documents. If you're in love with someone you have to register at their address, know what I mean?'

'But of course!' grandma beamed. 'Of course! No-one's disputing that! And he will register. First they'll get married, and then he'll register himself as living here. That's the proper procedure, isn't it?'

'What were you thinking about, though, taking him in like that when they weren't even married?' exclaimed the policeman. 'My ma would soon give any bloke his marching orders if he tried to shack up with my sister just like that! But here's you encouraging him... Supposing he does a bunk tomorrow?'

'He won't do a bunk,' whispered grandma with a glance over her shoulder at Matryona, who was standing sullen-faced and with arms akimbo in the doorway of the toilet, looking for all the world like the dishevelled evil witch of folk legend. 'Not him. They love each other, do you see?'

After a few moments of indecision the policeman gave two weeks' notice to register and departed. Then Matryona let rip.

'Lorst 'er brains, she 'as!' she barked, bringing her walking stick down on the floor so hard that the rubber plant shook. 'Let me tell it to yer straight — I ain't like that slut Katya what stole yer silver spoons. I tell yer by all that's 'oly, Lizaveta, it grieves me 'eart to see it! Such a lovely girl — like a swan, she is — and then to fall for a Yid! Yus, to 'ave 'im as 'er steady, damn his black 'eart! Yer'll never get them filthy 'eathen to accept yer as one o' their own! All that blood o' poor Christian folk as what they've drunk!'

My grandma never managed (I can hear it from here in Boston, thirty-five years later) — never managed to deliver a suitable riposte to Matryona, for at that very moment he himself appeared, shy and blue-eyed, in the kitchen: the curly-headed, muscular 'steady' with his clearly defined Semitic features. He had come in for a wash, and spent some time rinsing his hands and face in the ice-cold water, holding his brown hair under the tap while he was at it, so that water splashed all over the painted floor in the branching shadow of the rubber plant.

'Yer disgust me!' Matryona spat, and made herself scarce among her trunks and icon prints.

Now the sun burst forth triumphantly and with its August fire set about scorching the blue enamelled bowl on the stool, the bedraggled birch-twig besom under the sink and grandma's dainty hands as she dried the floor...

'Seen them all off!' she said to herself with a laugh. 'That clodhopper in uniform, and then the wicked witch!'

...Autumn is unusually colourful here in New England, where I live. The black tree-trunks are awash with golden foliage that stretches up and away into the vivid blue of a foreign sky.

As I walk along, I look down at my feet. I have just left work and am walking slowly, feeling tired and irritable. Suddenly I glance at the other side of the street and stop. I stand and watch. My father and my son are walking on the other side of the street. Clearly in a hurry, they are deep in agitated conversation as they walk. And although it is most likely some quite unassuming conversation on the subject of cars, my son is so excited that he runs on ahead to look his grandfather in the face. They both have exactly the same manner of walking, turning their toes in and moving their arms in the same way. What a mysterious thing heredity is! I watch them go until they disappear in the doorway, and I feel the clouds lift from my heart.

It was autumn too, all those thirty-five years ago. They were travelling to their dacha on an evening that glowed like wood-embers burning down in a stove. Outside the carriage window, trees glittered, awash with golden foliage; on wooden station platforms people were selling roasted sunflower seeds; and the wailing of an accordion mingled with blasts from the locomotive's whistle, both drifting off together into the red sky as a nervous trail of blue-grey smoke. There were not many people in the carriage. Suddenly she saw that he had turned pale and was clutching the top of his abdomen with both hands in the region of the solar plexus.

'What is it? What's wrong?'

'It hurts. Just here. O-oh!'

He writhed with pain on the wooden seat, and large beads of sweat appeared on his forehead below his neatly combed brown hair.

'But don't worry, it will pass soon. Soon it will be passing.'

His accent had become particularly pronounced, and his smart, dashing appearance had taken on something of a helpless child. Before her eyes he was changing into the startled Jewish youth she had seen on that faded photograph with its pencilled inscription in German: 'Grammar School No.7, Kaiser-Wilhelmstrasse, Class 6.'

'Are you feeling any better?' she sobbed, clasping his knees, which were locked together in a cramp.

'Yes, better. It's nothing to worry about. It has almost passed. I never told you: it began two months ago when he forbade me to see the boy. I was walking in Ulyanov Street, and the boy was looking at me from the window. I was leaving. I should have gone back to him, but I couldn't, I was going to you. And he was looking at me, looking at my back. And then, in the trolleybus, this started. Somehow I managed to get through the journey. And then the second time, do you remember when the boy was taken to hospital with scarlet fever? She made a telephone call and said I can go with him. I ran, but I came too late — they were already gone. I raced by taxi to that hospital — what is it called? — in Serpukhov Street. They were still at reception, and the boy rushed to me, trembling all over. He was in a long shirt with the hospital stamp on it. His grandfather had put it into his head that I am a bastard. A bastard, because I cannot live with his mother! But I am not a bastard, I am not!'

He pronounced the word with even more of an accent than the rest, using it (since expletives in another language always seem to have less force) to help him articulate his vague sense of being in the right.

'I did not meet his grandfather in the hospital — she said he was at the synagogue. He wouldn't have allowed her to ask me to the hospital. The boy was just trembling and clinging on to me. And then this woman — how do you call them? — this children's nurse seized him and took him away, but he broke free and ran back to me, and I embraced him again. And then they took him away again. He was shouting: "Daddy!" I took her home by taxi, and when I was walking back this pain started again. And now again. I rang them today, and they just put the

phone down. But I want to see the boy! Toma! Those bastards
— they are the pain!'

She stroked his damp forehead and murmured, 'Be patient,
it'll pass soon. It won't be long now, it's all nerves. We'll get out
at the next stop. It's just nerves, don't be afraid.'

A yellow-eyed old woman with a knapsack paused for a
moment in the gangway. 'Bless me, young fellow,' she said, 'are
you havin' a baby, or what, all doubled up like that! You oughta
see a doctor!'

At the platform he stood with his eyes closed and breathed
in the autumnal air with its slightly acrid smell of engine smoke,
squeezing her warm fingers and repeating: 'I am not a bastard, I
am not, I am not...'

An incandescent sphere rolled through the crunching snow
of First Workers' Street. The sphere was life itself — grinding up,
melting down and flattening eyes, words, hands, lips, innocence,
guilt. In its ascents and sudden downward stumblings was
everything that went to make up its days, hours and minutes: all
the component parts of its fiery burning flesh, its succulent apricot
softness, lurching across snow fallen overnight in First Workers'
Street.

Where its flesh bled were the terrified eyes of his child in
that long nightshirt that came down to his ankles, with 'Hospital
property' stamped across the middle; his cry of: 'Daddy!' splashed
like ink over the white hospital corridor that reeked of disinfectant.
Where it bled was the voice of his once father-in-law, so dry its
choking dust robbed him of breath: 'He's nothing to you now.
Don't come back here any more.' Where it bled were his hastily

packed suitcase, his hurried departure. But wherever she was, this same bleeding flesh was transformed into ripe apricot succulence, and where its sweetness trickled over his palate, down his throat and deeper, deeper — until all his innermost being burned with nothing but a pulsating happiness he could hardly contain — there would be her gentle voice in the mornings, her warm auburn locks on his shoulder, her warm shoulders with pink silken straps; and her jokes, her eruptions of suffocating laughter over evening tea, in the tranquil light of the orange lampshade.

Sometimes he would be taken aback in a rather naive way at the gentle ridiculing of life that went on all the time in this house, beneath the orange lampshade.

'Don't go in the kitchen — the professor's in there, giving a lecture,' her father would say, wrinkling his eyes, and grinning imperceptibly from behind his moustache.

This meant that Sashka — the janitor of Tatar origin who occupied the room next to Matryona's together with his wife Katya (a jealous woman of gigantic proportions, for marrying whom his hot-tempered Eastern kinsfolk had never ceased to curse him) — had once again gone into the kitchen to soak his feet in hot water and read the evening edition of *Pravda*.

'Pour in a bit more, Katya,' the man would say, crimson from the heat and moving his overdone legs up and down in the pail of hot water. 'Bloody stuff gets cold so quick, you don't seem to get any warmth from it. Anyway, listen to this about the plenary session.'

And he would start reading, one syllable at a time and all at the same unvarying pitch: 'The re-so-lu... re-so-lu-tion of the Par-... re-so-lu-tion of the Par-ty... bit more, Katya, don't be a Yid...re-so-lu-tion of the Par-ty on trans-gress-ors...'

'You are a terror,' Katya would mutter affectionately. 'Sittin' there in boilin' 'ot water, and then readin'! You'll ruin yer eyes — can't see a thing for all this steam! 'Ave yer gorn deaf, or what?'

Snow was falling slowly as they trudged back uphill from the squat brick bathhouse towards their home in First Workers' Street, feeling no less invigorated than Sashka from their steam bath.

'Do you think it's just by chance I've stayed here in this hole all my life, together with my wife and daughter? Why do you think I never said a word about getting a flat, never asked for anything? Never made any new acquaintances, never drank more than two glasses in other people's company? I was afraid of them, and still am. Basically, though, I don't give a damn for myself — *que sera, sera*. But I had to save Liza and Toma, and as far as I can see I've succeeded. I racked my brains: what could we do, where could we hide? And then I hit on it — just crept into this hole, as snug as a bug in a rug, and never stuck my nose outside again! Was anyone going to bother with the likes of me, a humble legal advisor? Just a minor civil servant, a real-life Akaky Akakievich... Of course not. Oh, I certainly wished for much better — but there's no point thinking about all that, is there? Of course not. Just look at how many people of my sort went under! They all wanted a normal life, they were attracted to the light. But out there in the light heads were falling like ripe apples. They still are. I used to dream at nights that they'd come to take me away. It wasn't even a dream as such, more — you know — a kind of mirage or hallucination. I'd see them taking me away, I'd be leaving the flat, but then at the door I'd suddenly look back, and there would be Toma standing by the stove, about thirteen years old, in her running shorts and vest. And I'd realize: this is it, the end. I quite often used to hallucinate like that. Sometimes I was afraid to go to bed and switch the light off. Of course, it was really an illness, but there was no doctor you could go to, was there, not with symptoms like that. Eventually it seemed to get better by itself, just faded away. What else can I say... The only indulgence I ever allowed myself was our dacha. I sold Liza's emerald necklace to get it built. You have to understand it was something I couldn't resist, something I'd really set my heart on. It was as if I'd managed by sheer cunning to claw back everything they'd taken from me. My estate may be gone, but now I have this little house and garden. And if I can't have a summer house with trellises, at least there's my bench underneath the jasmine. And forest all around, forest and fields. Going there from this hole with Sashka soaking his sweaty feet at nights is a real homecoming. There are cherry trees there, and nettles. The sound of cocks crowing, the smell of wood-smoke. If Toma has a little girl, I'll take her for walks in the forest, and we'll pick mushrooms.'

And with his slender hand he patted the younger man's shoulder, glistening in the lamplight beneath its coating of snow.

She woke him in the night. 'Please, I'm sorry, I won't bother you again. Just this once. I'm not going to die, am I? Suddenly I felt so afraid that I was going to die, and that you'd be left with a little girl to look after on your own, without me. Matryona would keep poking her with her walking stick.'

She was laughing, but her cheeks and chest were wet with tears.

'Don't talk such nonsense!'

On the other side of the wall Katya was snoring with a moaning sound. The beams from a car's headlights flicked smoothly across the ceiling.

'No, it's not nonsense, don't be angry. I suddenly had this feeling that it's going to happen. I won't be there, and you'll be left all on your own with a little girl...'

* * *

'Sit here for a while,' says my father, spreading his striped scarf over the sprinkling of snow on the little bench. 'I'll get some water for us to put the flowers in, then they'll last longer. They should stay fresh for four or five days.'

'Daddy,' I ask, peering intently at the pinkish stone and fine gold lettering, 'Daddy, where is she now? Can she see us, and the flowers? Can she see me sitting here?'

'Yes,' he says in a firm voice. 'Yes, she can see everything. She sees everything and knows everything.'

'But how?' I ask in surprise. 'How? Where is she?'

'She's up in heaven. She's our guardian angel. You know what that is, don't you? Well then, she's the guardian angel for both of us now.'

I do not understand everything he says, yet take it, as so many other things, on trust. While he fills a yellow-stained glass jar with water from the stand pipe and then cleans the headstone with a wet rag, I gaze up into the sky, seeing its cool blueness, and a frail little cloud, melting at the edges...

'Come on, let's go,' says my father. 'Otherwise you'll get cold.'

He wraps the striped scarf round his neck and lets me out

through the low little iron gate, then bends down to kiss the cold pink stone and slowly run his hand over it in farewell.

\* \* \*

On Fridays Matryona cooked pancakes. More often than not they got burnt, and you couldn't breathe for all the smoke in the kitchen.

'You get that down yer while it's nice an' 'ot!' she intoned. 'Look at this one bubblin' up! If you don't want it for yerself, eat it for that babby inside o' yer! When's it due? When yer've 'ad it, we'll see what that curly-'aired feller o' yourn is made of! It's when yer've got a babby an' it starts bawlin' its 'ead off at nights that yer menfolk start to show their true 'orrible selves. Then we'll see 'ow much 'e loves yer...'

Someone started knocking on the door, hammering away furiously on it.

' 'Oo the devil? Don't say it's them Tatars sozzled agin!' gasped Matryona, startled. She shuffled towards the door in her slippers.

First the corner of a battered black suitcase was pushed through the narrow door opening, and then Lala's round face, swollen with tears, bobbed into view above it.

'Oh, Toma, he's thrown me out! It's for real this time, Toma!'

She slumped down on a stool right there amidst the kitchen smoke and fumes and began sobbing out her despair in all its renewed vigour.

'Lala, please, come on, let's go into our room! Don't take on so! Lala, my dear, I'll go and see him straight away. Please don't take on so. Just think how many times he's thrown you out before! Don't upset yourself so. Just a minute, I'll get some valerian drops.

Thank God, here's Mummy now! Stay with her, you can see the state she's in. I'll be straight back.'

She slipped on her knitted jacket, which no longer buttoned over her stomach, and was gone.

He seemed not his usual self as he let her in. He was calm and sober.

'What do you want, Toma? You're all out of breath... Sit down. What is it?'

'Kolya, you're a decent person, I've always felt that. What's happened between you?'

'It's not something I really feel like discussing, Toma. But let's talk anyway, since you've come all this way in your condition. You said I was a decent person, right? Yet I can't even feel that I'm a person, just some sort of creature that lives from one day to the next, drinking, sleeping (usually with a woman because I'm scared to be on my own), guzzling vodka. And beyond that, an emptiness that's sort of black and clinging like the earth in a dug-out, with no ray of hope in the darkness. What can you expect from someone like that?'

'Kolya, please, try to understand her feelings!'

'It's my own feelings I'm trying to understand, Toma. I find it — how shall I put this? — I find it hard to get on with her. Poor girl, she's always trying to pull me up to the surface, whereas I want to dig down the other way, deeper and deeper into the earth. Well, it was my mistake, I didn't think things through properly. You know, she's like that poor little canary I had, twittering away and preening her feathers just the same. The best of all the women I've had, if truth be told. So affectionate you feel you want to cry. Only that doesn't alter anything. Whichever way you look at it, things can only get worse the longer we stay together. After all, what she needs is to have children, like you, and visitors around the place — the kind of life people normally have. Whereas me, I'm just happy to hit the bottle and keep that front door locked and bolted. What sort of a couple is that? Quite apart from which, I don't know how to love. Lost the knack, apparently. She'll be twittering away, and there's me choking with rage. I'm nothing more than a blight on her life. You've only to look at how she's changed! When she first came to me, she was like a vixen from the wild, all warm and fluffy. And full of laughs. And what does she look like now, four years later? A poor bedraggled cat. I should be feeling sorry for her and stroking her permed hair, instead of which I'll be seething like a samovar with anger. No, that's no sort of life for anyone, and there's really no point our discussing it any further. But since you're here anyway, perhaps you could do me a good turn and take all these fancy clothes with you, and all these little animals and dolls as well. Look at what she's turned this room into — more like a handicraft museum than somewhere to live! Although... I have to admit I'll miss her. Still, there's enough women around to see me through. They'll even go for a man with one leg. Ready to tear you apart with their teeth, they are, they're so hungry for it. You'd best be going now, Toma. I'm sorry that's the way things are.'

Slowly she walked down the stairs, thinking, 'How on earth am I going to tell her all that?'

Like some huge red tassel, the rowan tree was ablaze. Just that: ablaze. And the leaves were falling. I was born on the twenty-first of September. That morning a fire broke out in the wooden house opposite. There were flames shooting out of windows, the hissing of water; and there was I, asking this world to receive me, to let me in, while a pain more searing than any fire racked my mother's body. Then, a week later, I was received into that warm room in flat 4, No.4, First Workers' Street, and my fussy aunts (actually nieces of my grandfather) shouted at my father: 'No, no, don't put her down on the quilt, you have to put her on fur! That'll bring her health, happiness and prosperity!'

And so, his hands shaking with excitement, he laid me down on a shabby sealskin coat.

\* \* \*

'Come on now, drink up your milk while it's hot! My, there's no peace for the wicked! Shall I read you some more of *Eugene Onegin*? What do you want, then? Mummy's suitcase again?'

\* \* \*

She had sent an unexpected telegram: 'Return tomorrow eight. Carriage six. Natasha.'

Surprised and overjoyed, they went to meet her after three years' absence, her father clutching a bunch of wilting winter flowers. She felt cautiously for the steps with her foot as she alighted from the carriage, and came towards them, carrying her little girl in her arms.

'When she came to see us the next day,' said grandma, inobtrusively slipping a lump of butter into my hot milk, 'I couldn't believe my eyes! Absolutely stunning, she looked — a real Anna Karenina! She'd blossomed even more. Everything she had on was of foreign make. She had shoes with very high platform heels, I remember, and a jacket with wooden buttons. She'd had her hair cut short, too, although she had such lovely plaits before. But then any style suited her. When she saw you, she picked you up in her arms and wouldn't let go of you. My God, that poor woman...'

What did she tell my mother as they walked together through the glassy whiteness of Devichka Avenue? How would I know? I wasn't four months old yet, and I was asleep.

'I simply couldn't imagine any person I related to less, Toma. But now he's gone, I just want to bawl my head off, as Matryona would say. I'm on edge all the time, and I can't sleep. Although it's as if I can breathe easier now he's not around. There's not the same feeling of bitterness. Don't look at me so horrified like that! As it is you're the only person I can talk to about it. Well, anyway. I don't really know where to start. When we first got there, I felt physically sick. My head was spinning the whole time. It was more like a graveyard than a city, with everyone dressed in black, and polite blue-eyed children who never raised their eyes. The adults too, they never raised their eyes. He used to leave home at eight and come back at seven. He made it quite clear he didn't want me to have anything to do with the — what would you call them? — with the other wives... He was quite adamant: I was to stay at home and not even think about it — no confiding in anyone! Well, I was happy enough to go along with that. Those wives... Just moaning on all the time that they'd missed the boat, and there were no more rich pickings to be had! All the valuable tapestries had already gone, smuggled out in officers' suitcases. In fact they'd cleaned out everything in the first couple of years. So I stayed at home all on my own, and was sick.'

Suddenly she broke off. The snow drifting slowly down from the sky had whitened the knitted scarves over their heads and the unwieldy light-blue pram in which I lay asleep, hearing and understanding nothing of this snow-muffled conversation. She licked the snow from her upper lip, still saying nothing. And then my mother, pink from the cold, with tiny drops of water caught in her eyelashes, said to her, 'What? What is it?'

'I was sick, and all alone. He used to come back home in the evening. He changed a lot there — became very hard, somehow. He'd eat his meal without saying a word, and then...'

Again she fell silent. My mother waited fearfully.

'Then it was straight to bed. My God, you wouldn't believe the things he did to me! I was horrified at first, but then I got used to it. It was like being dragged down into a whirlpool, I had no will-power. Just thinking about it the next day made me go hot and cold all over. And what made it worse was that I was expecting Anya! I'd get up the next morning feeling awful, with marks all over my body and yet... how can I put it? Not happy, but as if somehow consumed by fire. No, please, I can't bear it, don't look at me. It went on like that for about three months, but then, when I was quite visibly pregnant, he suddenly went off me. He'd have his evening meal, read sometimes, and then off to bed and straight to sleep, without even giving me a kiss. He just couldn't be bothered. Then Anya was born, and I felt better straight away. For the first time I felt happy. And you know, Anya had this incredible resemblance to my mother right from the word go — it is amazing, isn't it? Somehow I even stopped taking any notice of him, I was so wrapped up in her. And I know this sounds preposterous and absurd, but it's true: he was jealous of her. Her cot was next to our bed, and I'd get up in the night to feed her. Like any other baby she'd cry a bit while I was changing her nappy, so naturally I'd take her into our bed and she'd be lying next to him. He didn't object to begin with, but then suddenly one night he threw a fit, shouting that he'd had a hard enough day's work without putting in a night shift as well, and if he'd known what a marvellous life I'd got lined up for him here, he'd have left me behind in Moscow for sure. So I got up to put Anya on the armchair — we had this big armchair, dark red, it was. But that made him wild too, because I'd done what he wanted so unquestioningly, you see — as if I'd considered it beneath me to argue with him, and done that deliberately to get at him. Even so, after Anya was born, and I was so exhausted I could hardly stay on my feet, he'd still wake me up nearly every night, and again I'd submit to him. Or rather, I must have loved him myself, with a dreadful, shameful kind of love. A debilitating, nocturnal, slavish love. It's impossible to explain, too embarrassing... Anyway, now I've told you practically all there is to know...'

Two completely white figures moving through the glassy wastes of Devichka. Behind the iron barrier: a tram, crawling like some snow-dusted caterpillar. And myself, asleep and dreaming.

The sky was packed with clouds like padding. The padding hung, heavy and tufted, above a little park where she sat next to a pallid, blue-eyed old woman in black mourning. The light was fading rapidly. She looked at her watch. Six o'clock: he'd be home for supper soon. Life was clattering along its well-worn tracks. The sky was packed with suffocating padding. She picked up the little girl with the dark complexion and gypsy looks and sat her in her pushchair.

'Come on, Anya,' she said. 'Daddy'll be home soon.'

The potato fritters stayed on the table, covered with a napkin, going cold. He didn't come home at seven, nor at eight, nor at nine. At ten she began to feel afraid. She paced back and forth through the three spacious rooms with their old oak furniture, her hands pressed to her temples, listening out for any sign. Perhaps he'd been sent on an urgent mission to the Western sector? But he usually got advance warning of these and told her he'd be away. Her second conjecture, wild as it was, was the one she held on to: another woman. That was it, no doubt about it. She took Anya into their bed and fell asleep, her face pressed against the little head with black curls. Towards morning she was woken by a knocking at the door. Two men in civilian clothes — one small and slit-eyed, with a lined face, the other tall and sinewy — pushed her aside and entered the flat without a word. Terrified, she pulled the flaps of her dressing gown tightly about her.

'Your husband didn't spend the night at home?' said the first man. It was more a statement of fact than a question.

'No,' she whispered. 'No, no...'

They asked her when he usually came home. She told them. The tall sinewy one suddenly removed his spectacles and put them in his pocket. His unblinking eyes, bare of eyelashes, looked across to where Anya was still sleeping.

'Did you notice anything odd or unusual about his behaviour yesterday?'

She managed to divert his gaze away from Anya. The smaller one with the lined face clicked his fingers.

'We're in no hurry. Take your time, try and remember...'

'What's happened to him?' she breathed. 'Where is he?'

'That we don't know yet. He was due to be debriefed on an important mission yesterday, but didn't report back. Just disappeared — without trace, apparently. So there you are. We've been searching for him all day and all night. Your hubby is nowhere to be found.'

And he suddenly gave her a familiar wink.

'This has led us to form certain suspicions,' resumed the tall sinewy one, polishing his spectacles. 'Which is why we have a few questions for you to answer now...'

She found the questions odd. Had he been studying a foreign language in the evenings? Not English, but an oriental language — Indonesian, for example? Or Japanese?

Had he been going on long country walks? How attached was he to his family? Eventually she couldn't take any more.

'Where is he, for heaven's sake?' she cried. 'What's happened to him?'

The smaller one patted her arm reassuringly.

'Our theory is that your hubby's done a bunk. Defected. Skedaddled!'

She shuddered. Anything else, but not that! What would happen to Anya?

'That's just our theory, don't forget — even if we do have certain grounds for believing it. But who knows, he might well have reported back for duty by this evening. Or again, someone might find an unidentified body lying in the woods, eh? Anything could happen...'

The sky was packed with clouds. The pallid old woman with straggling blue-rinsed hair looked on without interest as the little girl with the gypsy looks busied herself in the sandpit. It was all over. He wasn't coming back. But what about Anya, what would happen to her? Perhaps he was dead? Murdered? Killed by his own people, even? She suddenly remembered her father: 'They're just a pack, my dear: a pack of ravening wolves — hounds straining at the leash. Yet cunningly trained to attack their own kind more readily than others. Thirsting for kindred blood, you might say. Sowing terror all around, yet trembling themselves. A delightful picture. What do you have to say, my dear?'

The clink of the little blue decanter. Her mother's 'O-oh!'

That night she felt his hand impatiently caress her body, suffusing it with the usual familiar smouldering fire. 'Did you miss me?' The moist proboscis slipped between her lips, forcing them apart, insistent. He always started with that. 'Did you miss me?' She opened her lips and stretched towards him.

There was nothing there in front of her. She stretched, her lips open. The hand caressing her body became suddenly intangible. 'What do you have to say, my dear?' demanded her father's voice.

She opened her eyes. Transparent, like a lemon drop, the moon hung in the sky, held there as if by a miracle. Any moment now it would fall on her bed and spill its cool yellowness all over her. It was all over: he wasn't coming back. He'd defected. Or he was dead — killed by one side or the other, it was all the same. What was going to happen to Anya?

'I waited another few months, worried out of my mind, all on my own with my suspicions. Perhaps he was found out? Or he thought he'd be found out, and panicked? He might have defected, or he might have given himself up. Either side could have got rid of him. Officially they announced an internal inquiry, and I wasn't allowed to leave while it was in progress. Eventually they issued me with a document stating that he was "presumed missing", and I was allowed to go.'

I was asleep. It was snowing. Devichka Avenue was completely blanketed with snow. My grandfather obviously had a secret of some sort; his eyes had taken on a particularly wily expression. Grandma waited patiently for Sashka, who was soaking his feet, to vacate the kitchen. It was time to bathe their little girl. Who did that Sashka think he was, sitting there like some pampered lord?

'Liza,' said my grandfather, 'We shall have to employ a maid.'

'A maid?' gasped grandma, her eyes wide with astonishment. 'What do you mean, a maid?'

'Just what I say: a maid,' my grandfather repeated firmly. 'A clean-living girl who doesn't thieve or drink, to do the cooking and help out with the baby. What they call a home help these days.'

'Hankering after the old times again,' sighed grandma. 'Why can't you just admit defeat?'

So it was that a new face appeared in flat 4, No.4, First Workers' Street. Her name was Valka, and she had come up to the big city from Kaluga province. Gradually it began to look more and more as if my grandparents had taken her on as an exercise in fostering. 'Eat up now, don't be shy,' said my grand–father kindly as they were having breakfast. 'Put some butter on it, or you'll end up so thin you'll have sawdust coming out of you.'

Valka clapped her hand to her mouth and was convulsed with giggles.

'Don't hold your hand in front of your mouth when you laugh,' commented grandma. 'It's not done — doesn't look very elegant.'

Valka dutifully complied. 'Sorry, Aunt Liz, I won't do it no more,' she said; then, jabbing her finger at a blue plate with a picture of Napoleon on it, asked: ''Oo's 'e, then?'

'My dear, that's Napoleon,' sighed granddad. 'The Napoleon... You know, you ought to prepare for the technical college entrance exam. No point letting the grass grow under your feet: you must get yourself an education.'

And he brought a dog-eared copy of *The History of the Communist Party of the USSR* home from work with him. In the evenings, when she had tired of chatting with her girl friends on the phone, Valka would stretch out on her camp bed behind the screen and yawn with such relish that her eyes began to water.

'Now Valka, come along, my dear,' granddad would exhort her. 'Time for your studies.'

'Ooh, Uncle Kost',' said Valka, stretching herself with a clicking of joints, 'I'm dead-beat, that I am. I been pushin' the pram round the park for three hours, then I done the shoppin', and then this evening they had cotton print on sale in Zubovskaya

Street, an' I queued up for ages to get some for a dress. Me brain just won't take nothin' in, Uncle Kost'!'

'Then at least go over what you did yesterday again, my dear,' granddad appealed to her in desperation.

'Yesterday?' Valka sounded surprised. There was a rustling of pages. 'Ah, here we are: "The constitution is the basic law..." '

'But you've been learning that same sentence for a month now!' said grandma, her patience at an end. 'The constitution, over and over again!'

'The constitution is the basic law,' muttered Valka as she drowsed off. 'Basic law... constitution...'

And the weighty tome slipped to the floor. There it lay, gathering dust.

It was terrible to see Natasha in such a state. Her little Anya had been taken to the isolation hospital and was in the infectious diseases ward on the ground floor, where parents were not admitted. Natasha would pile up some broken bricks and stand on them, her face pressed to the half-whitewashed window, never taking her tearful, distraught eyes off the pinched little face on the shallow pillow. This continued for ten days. On the eleventh Anya died.

'No!' Natasha screamed, writhing convulsively on the freshly-washed tiled floor. 'No! I don't believe you, it's not true! Why don't you let me see her! I don't believe you!'

At the funeral she did not shed a tear. But when it was all over, she threw herself down on the fresh mound of earth and lay there motionless. They could do nothing to move her. Then my grandfather said to my mother, 'Go on, now, and take the others with you. Wait for us in the street.'

For a long time they stood, cold and tearful, waiting by the cemetery gates. At length she appeared, supported by my grandfather, her face smeared all over with earth.

At the beginning of 1953 my father lost his job in a programme of staff cutbacks which clearly presaged a major campaign against the Jews.

'Don't worry about it,' my grandfather comforted him, patting the back of his curly head. 'Let them choke on their own venom. We won't die of hunger.'

'I'll get a job as a hammerer!' said my father through clenched teeth. 'Look at these muscles!' He flexed his bronzed arm, and the muscles came up as hard as rocks. 'I'll go and work in a factory. The bastards!'

'Yes, it's easy to keep your head down in a factory,' said my grandfather with a melancholy grin. 'A nice safe job...'

Then, in March, came the death of our bewhiskered leader. Valka lay all dishevelled on her camp bed, keening. The rissoles were burnt. Crowds pushed and jostled in the streets.

'Nobody is to go outside the house today,' said grandfather, his finger raised in admonition. 'Nobody.'

'What!' squealed Valka. 'Are you all there, or what, Uncle Kost'? What about payin' our respects?'

'Do as you're told and stay there!'

His face was inscrutable.

...I am lying on the sofa with my favourite doll. The doll is called 'Korean Pak': a yellow, slit-eyed boy in baggy trousers of blue silk. There is a knock at the door. Mummy's come home!

'Hurry,' grandma whispers to me. 'Take Mummy's slippers to her.'

Whenever anyone asked me, years later, 'Can't you remember her at all?' I would always reply, 'Yes, I can. I remember her coming home from work, and me taking her slippers to her.'

\* \* \*

...Mist. The milk-white mist of my clumsy childhood memory, through which I wander, feeling my way with outstretched hands, blundering into my own dreams and the reminiscences of others. And suddenly in this whiskery mist that hisses like blood in the ears, my outstretched fingers come up against something solid and tangible, something fluffy: my mother's slippers. A pair of red slippers. Yes, they were real, I know that for sure.

...I am crawling under the sofa to get the slippers, then I hear someone laughing, and I run towards her. I can't actually see her. All I feel is an incredible lightness, combined with something bright and radiant that bends down over me, a warmth that brushes my head and then vanishes. God, this mist... I can't see a thing. And then?

...pillows, a mass of pillows. I draw closer, and again something large and radiant comes floating towards me. I hear no laughter.

'Mummy's not well,' my grandma whispers. 'Come on. Mummy's asleep.'

But she is not asleep. I clearly see something white (her hand?) gliding to brush aside an auburn-coloured wave (her hair?) on the large white pillow. She is not asleep: she is sitting up, leaning back on the pillows, and her hair is in the way. Again everything breaks off abruptly. Milk-white mist, hissing like blood in the ears, through which I wander with outstretched arms...

\* \* \*

There was a sheaf of papers in a brown suitcase, bundled up separately from the rest. It was with various official documents and had never struck me as being of particular interest. But when I did after all untie it one day, my eye was immediately caught by some very odd phrases: '...my wife... the scurrilous accusation made against my wife... died in March 1955... Dear Mr Khruschov, I appeal to you... I am convinced that this breach of legality, and the outrageous slur on her character which drove her to her death...'

Four months had passed since the death of little Anya. Lala was sitting by the fire on a little low bench. Her hair had grown noticeably darker. Natasha was wrapped in a shawl. Outside, snow was falling thick and fast.

'Is it tomorrow you start work?'

'Yes,' said Toma. 'I'm a bit nervous. But you should see the carpets they've got there, and the mirrors. It's a palace! No, really! I thought I wouldn't like it there, but it's all right. Quite nice, in fact. The typists all wear patent-leather shoes. God only knows where they get them from! Imported, I shouldn't wonder.'

'Where are you flying to, Toma my dear?' There was a clink of the little blue decanter from the next room. 'Into a wasps' nest, that's where... But you're not a wasp, my dear, you're a butterfly, a chocolate brown...'

'She's very keen on English, Daddy,' said Natasha quietly, wrapping her shawl more tightly about her. 'She won't be getting involved in anything, just interpreting during negotiations. After all, the Ministry of External Trade isn't the Ministry of Internal Affairs, and you shouldn't confuse the two.'

'My dear, in this country all affairs are "internal", there is nothing "external". And not to get involved with them — that's impossible. We're all involved with them. Even an old soak like me — just by accepting them and saying nothing. Oh, Toma! You'd do better to stay at home and take your little girl for walks in the park...'

Watched over by a frowning granite Tolstoy, Valka was taking me for a walk in the park. She was chattering away nineteen to the dozen with her friends, and had I been a little older I should have had no difficulty understanding what was going on in our house.

'I shall be startin' at Technical College in a year's time,' Valka trilled. 'I can't leave 'em just yet, Auntie Liz couldn't cope without me. They're all off to work at the crack o' dawn, all goin' their separate ways: Toma in one direction, Uncle Kost in another, and Curlylocks in another. They've taken him back translatin' them books again, you know. He knows all the languages there is to know! When I used to live in the country, I thought all Jews was sort of old and blue-looking, like battery hens. I'd got this stupid idea their fingers was all crooked and tough, and they'd grab hold of you if you didn't watch out. Old Grandma Klavdya used to say to me: "You beware o' the Yids, Valka, more'n anything else! If you catch sight of a Yid, just turn tail an' don't look back!" But that's really all a load o' codswallop, girls — ours is a fine figure of a man. He washes himself in cold water twice a day, God's honour, an' he loves our Toma to death! Don't drink, neither — never touches a drop, God's honour! He's very hot-tempered, though: that's his only fault. If summat's not to his likin', he can really fly off the handle! But it soon passes. She'll stroke his head, an' before you know it he's all right again. He didn't hit it off with his first wife — I s'pose she never found the right way to handle him. But our Toma's clever: she never answers him back, but still she always gets her own way. God gave her brains, all right, an' that's the truth, girls...'

After giving birth she had unexpectedly put on weight. Invariably late, she would run to Smolensk Square (this was quicker than relying on the infrequent trams) and, arriving out of breath, push open the heavy door. After showing her pass and shaking the snow from her knitted scarf, she would take the lift to the ninth floor, to be greeted by the smell of ink, paper and strong tea and the sight of typists pounding the keys with their dark-red nails.

'...she was simply in love with her work,' says my father with an anguished expression, 'She liked everything about it: that twenty-storey monstrosity with its towers, all that rushing around, having to speak English all the time... How dearly she paid for her vanity!'

Just after New Year a new head of department was appointed.

'Lala,' she exclaimed, clasping Lala's head between her hands, 'how I wish you could get to know him! He's such a wonderful person, so considerate. Somehow I just know he's not married!'

'...she was always full of somebody or other,' says my father with the same anguished expression. 'Always had to be mother hen to somebody, making matches, arranging meetings. Terrible! You're just the same, and that's what I'm afraid of!'

'...my wife was accused to her face of having an illicit affair with her head of department, Comrade Ryzhov,' I read on the sheet of paper, now yellowed with the passage of years. 'My wife (*deletion*)... to endure these quite undeserved smears and (*deletion*)... after her subsequent dismissal took to her bed...'

'Drink your milk! I don't remember anything! I don't want to remember it. Ask your father: let him tell you about it if he sees fit. Drink it up while it's hot...'

How did it all begin? I would hardly know, would I? Valka was taking me for a walk in Devichka Avenue, where a stern-looking Tolstoy had his eyes fixed on me.

Out of breath, she pushed open the heavy door and showed her pass. There was an unusual buzz of excitement in the department. Typists were whispering in corners.

'Ryzhov's in trouble. He's been called upstairs.'

'What for?'

'He was guilty of ideological error during yesterday's

negotiations, Toma. He said production of agricultural machinery still hadn't recovered from wartime losses, and...'

'But what's ideological about that?'

'Are you joking? Anyway, you were interpreting at the time, weren't you? Didn't you notice anything?'

'What absolute nonsense!' she exploded. 'Where is he? In his office?'

He was seated behind his desk with its battery of telephones. There was a look of despair on his pasty face.

'I'm in trouble, have you heard?' he said, massaging his temples with the palms of his hands. 'I've taken a couple of painkillers, but it's no good, I've got a splitting headache. What a business...'

'But my dear Dmitry Stepanych, I was interpreting! I remember the context! The way you said it, it didn't sound at all out of place!'

'Toma,' he said, lowering his voice and glancing over his shoulder with a hunted look on his face. She involuntarily moved closer to hear what he said. 'They'll kick me out in the next day or so, I've no illusions about that. Let's just hope it's nothing worse... Thank you for coming to see me.'

And then her heart began to pound. I hear it pounding uncontrollably: her heart, in which that defect qualified as 'latent' had lain dormant, revealing in this latent guise no sign of itself until the appointed time, until its hour had come.

'Why are you so short of breath, Toma my dear?' asked my grandfather, closely scanning her burning face as they drank their evening tea. 'What are you so upset about?'

'I've just been telling you! The sheer injustice of it — and what makes it worse, it was me interpreting!'

'You burn with indignation as though you enjoyed the good fortune of being able to take justice for granted. But that's something you can whistle for in this country!'

'I know, but it was me interpreting!'

Her face was burning, and she was panting for breath.

Two days later Ryzhov was dismissed, and his place behind the desk with its battery of phones was taken by his deputy, a small fidgety man with pebble glasses.

'But I can't accept it, I can't! How can I just not say anything? You should have seen the way he left: he was a broken man. As he was going out of the door, he dropped a book and apologized, and they all just sat there stony-faced. My God, there could be people being robbed, killed, crucified, and no-one would dare speak up!'

'You do know, don't you,' whispered my father, 'how it would all have ended if he were still alive? That's something, at least. Relax. You can't change the world single-handed, you know. Go to sleep now.'

He went to sleep before her, and she lay with her eyes open as the light from occasional car headlights flicked smoothly across the low ceiling, her face burning, her heart pounding. I was asleep in the next room.

Over my cot hung a woven rug on which a fiery-red fox held a ruffled white cockerel gripped between its teeth, dragging it off to its deep lair, beyond the blue forest, over the hills and far away...

She wrote a letter which nobody signed apart from her. Naively, she wanted to see justice restored; although justice (as surely she knew?) had always been something you could whistle for. During those days she started taking the tram to Smolensk Square, as yet not even consciously aware that she just didn't have the strength to run. She was short of breath, and at nights she was troubled by a persistent cough. 'Have you caught a cold?' my father asked anxiously. After a few days she was summoned to the fidgety deputy head's office.

'What made you think you could fire off letters of support without being in full possession of the facts? I've had a phone call from some colleagues demanding that I look into the matter. Such a fervent letter you write, so lyrical — but to be blunt, completely lacking in substance and foundation. An idiotic letter, in short. What's more, I suspect personal motives at work here. And as you know...'

'What did you say?'

Her heart pounded in her throat.

'I merely said what's already common knowledge. Ours is a government department, as you well know, not some piffling office dealing with housing problems or firewood stocks. So we shall not stand for anyone introducing what one might call artistic licence of this sort into the work of the department.'

His pebble glasses glinted at her point-blank.

'How dare you talk to me like that!'

'Dare?' He raised his voice, lifting himself half-way out of his heavy upholstered chair. 'Dare? How dare you, employed in a Soviet department of state, try to cover up for your fancy men with your idiotic scribblings, just tell me that!'

She flew out, slamming the door behind her, then sat down on the nearest chair and started coughing. That afternoon she was summoned to the personnel department. Her letter of dismissal was already signed.

The snow has been melting. Sunlight dazzles the windows of the bus, filled with the smell of petrol fumes, in which my father and I are travelling. I feel my frenzied heart struggling to burst free from my throat as I ask him indignantly: 'But how, how could she get so upset that it made her ill and she died? How? She had me, didn't she? Or didn't she love me?'

My face is burning, and I pant for breath, my nose pressed hard against the window, which is covered with driblets from the springtime thaw.

'You're thirteen years old,' he says wearily, 'yet you talk like a little child. Nobody forgot about you. Until she was affected by this lousy system herself it was hard for her to imagine just how lousy it is. She lived with her head in the clouds until her eyes were opened by that whole squalid, idiotic business. It's really quite amazing. To grow up in a family like hers and then, when it comes to the crunch, to be found so helpless and naive — that is incredible, quite amazing! And yet it all really distressed her so much that she couldn't think about anything else. She burned herself out. After all, it doesn't take much for a weak heart...'

He falls silent. The bus smells of petrol; sunlight dazzles the windows.

She has stopped going to work. The red slippers sit forlornly by her bed, where she sits propped up on a mass of pillows,

coughing. Valka and I come in; logs are burning in the stove, and
there is a smell of medicine in the room. We are covered with a
powdering of snow, and our faces glow pink. Through the window
yard-sweepers can be seen clearing the snow. She brushes a heavy
lock of auburn hair from her face and asks Valka, 'Is it cold outside?
Shouldn't she be wearing warmer clothes?'

Natasha follows us in, thinner than she was, and looking
stern, and says calmly, 'It's beautiful outside, there's a smell of
spring in the air. Time you got better!'

She coughs.


I am making a snowman, watched over as ever by Tolstoy.
Valka is sitting on a sledge, surrounded by her friends.

'Toma gave me her astrakhan hat yesterday,' she sobs. ' "I've
got to stay in bed anyway," she says, "and the winter'll be over
and done by the time I'm better. You wear it." So she gave it to
me. She's coughin' her poor heart out. We had two doctors in
yesterday — professors, both of 'em, in private practice. Uncle
Kost went by taxi to fetch 'em. They said it's her heart, but you
tell me, girls: who gets a cough from heart trouble? I reckon they
just make it up to swindle folk out of their money! The other
mornin' I had to go to the toilet — just gettin' light, it was — an'
I see Uncle Kost sittin' on a stool in the kitchen. Sittin' there with
his head in his hands, cryin', he was. We all live in fear. We sit
down for our supper, and the food just sticks in our throats.
They're doin' some final tests tomorrow, and then they'll decide
whether she has to go into hospital, or what...'


With his slight frame and sad Jewish profile, the old doctor stood for a long time, shaking snow from his galoshes. Katya glided regally past them, carrying a plate of lopsided buns to her room.

'May I wash my hands?' he said, raising his eyebrows with an air of sadness, and went through into the kitchen. My father followed him with a towel. He was so agitated that his accent had become more pronounced again.

'She's been through some very unpleasant business at work and taken it very hard. It's made her take to her bed. Please, speak to her as a specialist, tell her that...'

'We have no remedies to offer for life, my dear fellow,' said the doctor, his mournful eyes encountering my father's anxious gaze. 'Especially the kind of life we have to lead...'

She was coughing as, frowning, he held his stethoscope to her chest, tapped her ribs and took her pulse...

'The local social security officer called me a malingerer this morning,' she laughed, brushing the auburn waves from her face. 'He said it was to my advantage to be ill. I wonder how that could be?'

'Ill-bred louts,' he smiled at her. 'Don't take any notice. You mustn't be so quick to take everything to heart: your heart doesn't appreciate it.'

...How had he survived, this thin little old doctor, the only one to realize how seriously ill she was? How had he, with his mournful brown eyes, managed to hold on until the relatively good times of 1955?

'Only one person actually suspected what was later confirmed by the post-mortem — and he wasn't even a professor, just an ordinary hospital physician,' says my father with an anguished expression. 'He'd just returned from the camps, just been given clearance to practise again. Little old chap he was, Jewish. He was really frowning after he'd examined her, and he told us...'

What did he tell them?

They were standing round the table, waiting: my grand-parents and my father. He stood in thought for a moment, frowning, and then said, 'It's serious. She needs to go into hospital — at once, without delay. Strange that she hasn't been hospitalized already. Ring my office in the morning: I'll try to get her admitted there tomorrow. She'll have to be operated on, I'm afraid.'

He looked sadly into my father's eyes, which were darting back and forth.

'Don't leave her on her own tonight. Stay with her, in case anything happens...'

She died that night.

Mist. Dry-eyed, I wander through mist. I am alone; she is not there. Through the foreshortened years I grope my way towards her: through an endless recurrence of mist, mist, mist, a mass of white pillows, red slippers, light...

'...my wife was not in poor health... Three years before her sudden death she gave birth to a perfectly healthy child, successfully and without complications...'

My father and I are on a bus. The sun is dazzling.

'Just tell me: if it hadn't been for that, would she have lived?'

The unbearable thought takes my breath away: if it hadn't been for that, she would have...

There were a lot of people in the church. Inquisitive old women crowded near the entrance, whispering among themselves: 'She was very young, twenty-five or thereabouts. Married, too: that's her husband, the one with the curly hair. O -oh! There's no escaping fate!'

And I? I had no idea of any of this. Valka, her face puffy from crying, had taken me for a walk. While the office for the dead was being sung and they took their final farewell of her, I was making a snowman from March's last remaining snow. While my father gazed at her, his eyes never leaving her altered face, I was searching for my spade in a prickly snowdrift. That night Valka and I stayed with friends of the family.

'She were an angel, a real angel,' said Matryona mournfully in the kitchen. 'An' God always takes 'is angels to 'isself. Needs to 'ave them near at 'and, you see... What's the point o' them bein' down 'ere, just slavin' away for 'eathens, Lord forgive me, sinner that I am!'

Indeed. But why did Lala and Natasha disappear from my life too, at the same time as my mother?

'I'm going to stay here. Just for tonight,' said Lala to Natasha, who was standing motionless, dressed all in black. The funeral meal was over; they had washed the dishes and cleaned the floor. 'You go home. I'll stay.'

And so Natasha left, and Lala stayed. She slept on the camp bed in the room soon to be renamed Daddy's room. No sound came from the small adjoining room to which my grandparents had withdrawn. My father said nothing, while she sobbed, her face buried in the pillow. Then she started trying to comfort him, although he continued to say nothing.

'I'll always be there for you and your little girl,' she sobbed. 'We'll bring her up together. We'll bring her up, just as if Toma were still alive. I'll be there for you both, do you hear? Is there anyone else in the world I care more for?'

Towards morning she fell asleep. She was woken by the door creaking. In the dull white light of dawn stood my grandma, dressed as she had been the day before, and my grandfather, his suit fastidiously buttoned up, looking between them like two elongated, ghostly shadows.

'Go home, Lala,' said grandma in an even voice. 'I don't want to see either of you: you or Natasha. She's gone, and I don't need anyone else. I'll manage on my own. She came to me and asked me not to abandon her little girl — came to me in a dream. I gave her my word. I don't need anyone else. I didn't want to go on living, but she begged me with tears in her eyes. So it'll be as she wishes. Go now, Lala. I don't want to see either of you: you or Natasha.'

She turned and left. Without a word, my grandfather went across to Lala, kissed her on the parting of her dark hair, and also left.

What snow! Like cotton wool soaked in water, everything falls apart under the touch of my mittens. A ruffled sparrow in a white bonnet hops from twig to twig. Voices sound softer and slower, floundering in this blinding white pulp together with my felt boots, the sparrow's claws and my father's pointed-toe shoes.

We are hurrying to the theatre. Could I ever have the audacity to say before I die that I have not known happiness in this life, when in my sixth year I was vouchsafed that snow-smothered Sunday morning, a new dress with a lace collar, and the plush red velvet of the theatre box — which we entered, late as usual, only after the lights had dimmed, so that I failed to notice the pretty woman with black eyebrows and piled-up plaits, her face lit by a radiant smile?

The children trudge across the stage, searching for the Blue Bird. I find it interesting, if somewhat disconcerting, that their dead grandparents talk to them as if still alive from their vantage point on a piece of thick white lace vaguely resembling a cloud. My grandma and grandfather are alive and will never die, and are waiting for me at home. The theatre is warm and dark, and scented with perfume and oranges. My new dress with its lace collar is the prettiest in the whole world. The lights go up for the interval. The slim, pretty woman with black eyebrows, her eyes brimming with unshed tears, kisses me and clasps my head tightly to her bosom. Daddy reminds me that her name is Natasha. She looks at me all the time — joyfully and eagerly, as if feasting her eyes. Then we go to the refreshment bar, where my eyes run wild at the sight of so many different-coloured cakes. But no, I decide I'd rather have some chocolate — the one with all the Pushkin fairy tales on the wrapper: the oak-tree with the chain on it, the old man with his fishing net, Ludmila in her elaborate head-dress, and the talking cat... Afterwards we travel, or rather sail, through slowly-gliding whiteness, past dreary chimney smoke and glassy trees — sail on and on, to disembark at a semi-basement room with snow-white net curtains at the window and a round table with a snow-white cloth laden with pastries, sweets, cups of various sizes, and napkins embroidered with doves and forget-me-nots. Two plump, portly old ladies like ducks are fussing about the table, as well as a round-faced woman with curly hair and raised eyebrows who drops everything as soon as she sees me and smothers my head in its cold, frost-whitened hood with kisses, clasping it to her bosom just as Natasha had done. We drink tea, and I take a closer look at this room with its photographs on the walls, its dark, creaking sideboard, its wicker armchair with protruding osiers...

While I eat a pastry, the assembled women look on, never taking their eyes off me. The nose of one of the plump, duck-like old ladies turns comically red at the tip, and tears roll down her cheeks...

'God grant that you have friends like that,' says grandma gravely, carefully replacing the photographs in their rice-paper wrapping. 'You're not drinking your milk again! Drink it up now, while it's hot...'

# Philemon

## and

## Baucis

*Philemon and Baucis, husband and wife in Ovid's*
Metamorphoses, *entertained Jupiter and Mercury*
*disguised as travellers. In gratitude Jupiter offered*
*to grant any wish they might have. They asked*
*that they might die on the same day, and their*
*wish was granted. After death Philemon turned*
*into an oak and Baucis into a linden, and their*
*branches intertwined at the top.*

*From:* Brewer's Dictionary of Phrase & Fable

I

*I*n a dacha outside the city lived Philemon and Baucis. In the mornings the sun came filtering in through heavy curtains, to scatter in hot patches of light over Philemon's bulldog chin, sagging open as he slept, and the pleated folds of his neck; then, slipping away towards the other bed on the left, it found Baucis's gnarled, skinny hand stretched out on the silk eiderdown and lit up her fingernails, veins and brown age spots, before creeping on up towards her open mouth with its fringe of black hairs, where, losing all interest in the sleeping couple, it gave a sardonic grin, faded and left the room. Next a grunting sound would be heard. She was always the first to wake up: wiping away a dribble of saliva with the palm of her hand, she would take an anxious look at the snoring Philemon to make sure he was still alive before hurriedly thrusting her swollen feet into a pair of worn slippers and setting about the business of living.

She scurried about at her tasks with a sense of urgency, for by the time Philemon was awake she would have to prepare breakfast, fetch water and clean the veranda (dirt was something she could not abide). There had been a heavy downpour overnight, the clay paths were treacherous, and, anxious not to fall, she stepped warily in the rubber galoshes she had slipped on her bare feet, leaning to her right, where in a tall enamelled pail icy, limpid water slopped back and forth from her awkward movements.

'Zhenya!' eventually came the quavering tones of Philemon's voice. 'What time is it?' 'Ten o'clock already, Vanya,' she replied, half-opening the door from the veranda. 'Time to get up. Is your headache better?' 'Better just check,' he said, clearing his throat. 'God helps those who help themselves,' she clucked soothingly, perching on the edge of his bed to fit the black rubber sleeve of the blood-pressure gauge round his arm. Then they both held their breath, Philemon's bulldog chin trembling slightly with frailty. 'Well, that's all right, then,' came her sigh of relief. 'You're doing just fine: a hundred and forty over eighty. Now come and have your breakfast — they'll be bringing Alyona soon.'

Three years previously their younger daughter Tatyana had given birth to a large pallid baby. Tatyana was unmarried. She had turned out so like her father, with the same bulldog looks, that for a long time no man had shown the slightest interest in her. But eventually she had come back pregnant from a tourist trip to Hungary and Czechoslovakia.

'He'd damn well better marry her, the swine!' thundered Philemon. 'Otherwise I'll have his guts for garters — have him kicked out of the KGB, the son-of-a-bitch! His feet won't touch the ground... Think they can run rings round us, his sort!'

But time passed, and Tatyana remained unmarried. The later stages of pregnancy found her pounding away on her typewriter at nights and disappearing in the library for hours on end; and a month before the baby was due she was awarded her master's degree and landed a senior teaching post at the polytechnic. Presumably this gave the KGB officer with the small premature bald patch and fastidious expression pause for thought, for although he did not marry her, neither did he exactly go out of his way to avoid her. Tentative talk of a three-room flat in a housing co-operative would sometimes fall from his impassive lips; and two days after the birth of their child he turned up at the maternity unit bearing some greasy-looking defrosted strawberries in a plastic bag.

They called their little girl Alyona. The older she grew, the less her fairy-tale name seemed to suit her. Tatyana, unbalanced by her maternal instincts, force-fed poor Alyona like a guinea-pig in some bizarre experiment. At the age of three she looked like a six-year-old, and they had to buy her clothes in the young schoolchildren's section of the Children's World department store. To an accompaniment of songs, exhortations, toys, books and rattles they would seat this pasty-faced creature at the table, decked out in enormous ribbons and snugly wrapped in a towel, then cram into her reluctant mouth caviar on rolls, morsels of calves' liver, and blackcurrants mashed up with sugar, all washed down with thick carrot juice. Swathed in towels, Alyona would attempt to resist, giving voice to deep-throated howls and kicking out at the high chair with her thick-set legs. 'Watch the little birdie flying there,' Tatyana would appeal to her. 'And now let's catch him — yum!' Choking, Alyona would bring up everything she had eaten; and straight away they would wash her, dress her in clean clothes, spread new caviar on new rolls, pulp knobbly fresh carrots in the screeching electric juicer.

'Get up now, Vanya,' said Baucis on days when their granddaughter was expected. 'They're bringing Alyona today.'

'Are they?' exclaimed Philemon, agreeably startled. 'So we'd better get down to the market, eh Zhenya?'

'Yes, let's go before it gets too hot. Or you stay at home, and I'll go on my own.'

'No, I'll come with you, there's no need to go on your own,' he quavered. 'Uh-huh-huh...'

She made sure he remembered to take all his medicines, and squeezed drops of imported lotion into his bleary, bulging eyes for him, then crawled under the bed with her enormous chapped heels spread apart and spent some time rummaging around in search of his crêpe-soled ankle boots. They set off for the market together, she, like him, greeting acquaintances with much ceremony, commenting with approval on the weather, asking after people's health, cooing over babies in prams, and even chuckling like him: 'Uh-huh-huh, huh-huh...'

Sometimes Philemon flew into fits of rage. She was afraid of these, any one of which could easily end in a stroke. Some boys from the other dachas might be sitting on somebody's fence and breaking branches off a rowan tree. His face flushed purple, his stick with its heavy bronze handle held in the air, Philemon would rush at the fence, wheezing: 'I'll have you lot! Ruddy hooligans! I'll do for you, you scum!' Then, grasping his elbows from behind, she would urge him, 'Come on, Vanya, don't bother yourself with them! Va-anya!' Panting heavily, with whistling indrawn breaths, Philemon continued on his way to the station, gradually calming down as he went. 'What a rabble! What a bloody shower! I'd have the lot of 'em shot out of hand!' And again she sought to placate him: 'Of course, of course... Why sully your hands with them... You should think of yourself more.' 'There's no discipline, Zhenya!' Philemon lamented, still a pale shade of purple from his recent outburst. 'That's why you get that sort of behaviour — discipline's all gone to pot everywhere. People have got out of hand...' 'Shush, Vanya,' she hissed, instantly assuming a false, lopsided smile. 'Well, look who it is! It must be ages...' 'Uh-huh-huh,' Philemon chuckled, softening now, as he clownishly squirmed with incoherent delight at the sight of some routine acquaintance with a shopping trolley. 'Well, well, look who's beaten us to it! Bet you haven't even left any blackcurrants for us at the market, eh? Uh-huh-huh...'

After lunch an official car would draw up outside the fence of their dacha. Alyona was delivered to her grandparents courtesy of Tatyana's boy friend. Tatyana — thin, with brittle bright-blond hair and thickset jaw — emerged from the car, staggering under the weight of her sleeping daughter, while they came running helter-skelter down the veranda steps towards her. 'Here's our little girlie and her mummy,' cooed Philemon. 'Get the table laid, Zhenya. Here they are, then. Who's brought granddad's little girlie to see him?' After she had eaten, Tatyana, feeling tired, picked berries in a low-cut summer frock or lay swinging in a hammock with the newspaper, while they filled a plastic bathtub with water, carried it out into the sunshine and between them, their hunched shoulders colliding, bathed pot-bellied, overfed little Alyona, who lay splashing soapy water over the sides with her chubby unwieldy hands, her blue eyes staring at the sky. In the evening Tatyana pencilled in her eyebrows, slapped on a thick layer of pink lipstick and rushed off to catch the train back into town, while they stayed with Alyona. Then Philemon read fairy-tales to her. 'I'd give birth, for our dear Tsar, to a hero famed afar,' he mumbled, nearly nodding off himself as he monotonously rocked her cot. Usually Alyona would start hiccuping noisily. 'Oh dearie me,' Philemon would fret. 'Bring us some juice, Zhenya — nice raspberry juice for our little girlie...'

When she had had enough raspberry juice and the hiccups had subsided, Alyona went off to sleep. Now Philemon opened his newspaper while she finished washing the dishes with her gnarled, flattened fingers. Thoughts came crowding into her head as she fought against fatigue: tomorrow she'd have to go to the market again (they'd forgotten to buy rhubarb, and Philemon's digestion was playing up!), wash out all Alyona's tee-shirts, and give the upstairs room a good clean, because on Friday Tatyana might not come on her own, but bring that evasive young man of hers. Then they'd have to do their utmost to give them a taste of happy family life, with a slap-up meal, and their baby girl all spick-and-span and hiccuping from all the goodies they'd fed her, so as to give that indecisive fellow with the premature bald patch and impassive lips the firm impression that this was his home, his dacha, his wife and daughter.

'Damn me,' Philemon wheezed, shaking his grizzled, trembling fist at something in the newspaper. 'Damn me, there'd have been none of this in the Boss's day! They'd have bloody well had the whole damn pack of 'em shot out of hand!' He raised his bleary eyes, swimming with imported lotion, to the small portrait framed in funereal black. With its large nose and black moustache, buttressed from beneath by the stiff collar of a military-style jacket, the face peered back at Philemon through narrowed lids with an affectionate, crafty expression. 'Uh-huh-huh,' Philemon sighed, feeling calmer now. 'Uh-huh-huh...' He lowered his voice. 'Zhenya, I think I should report that Jew: he gets hold of foreign newspapers to read. And that's just for starters, 'cos even worse, he listens in to Western radio stations. You can hear everything from their veranda. If they think they can put one past me... We should report them...' She was holding her fingers apart as she dried them with a clean towel. 'Think of yourself, Vanya!' she said. 'You've done your bit. Anyway, where could you report them to these days?'

Deep down she felt that at the time Philemon had done the wrong thing in zealously upholding the ideals of his Communist youth and refusing to accept that any errors at all had been committed during a certain period of recent history. Now in their old age, thanks to this fanatical obstinacy of his, they had no chauffeured official car to call their own, no daily domestic help, no dacha in the government countryside resort. They did, it was true, have a one-bedroom flat on Kutuzovsky Avenue, a good pension, exclusive hospital treatment and special food parcels twice a month. Yet there were others — much smaller fry than Philemon, without long years of high-ranking service in the Uzbekistan Central Committee to their credit — who had more than them! And she looked with compassion at her honourable, uncompromising old man, sitting engrossed in his newspaper beneath that large-nosed, much lamented face, and thought that of course he was right again: they ought to report such goings-on. Yet with things as they stood nowadays you didn't know where to start. Who would you report them to? You could end up a laughing stock.

'Come to bed, Vanya,' she urged. 'Alyona might wake up in the night, and then we'll be worn out in the morning. We'll have to go to the market first thing, I haven't got anything for dinner yet... You can stay in the playground with her while I do the shopping...' Grunting, they lowered themselves into their beds with the identical silk eiderdowns. It never took Philemon more than a moment or so to start whistling through his fierce-looking pug nose. She would get up to straighten the pillow under Alyona's head, check the gas was switched off in the kitchen and the front door locked, then go back to bed. The moon, filtering through a crack in the curtains, licked at her sideways-drooping cheek with its tuft of long black hairs. Cool, jasmine-scented air came wafting in from the garden. A nightingale that had bided its time burst into song somewhere between heaven and earth; and to the sound of its untiring voice she would fall asleep.

One night she was woken by a high-pitched yammering sound. She opened her still unseeing eyes with a shock and sat bolt upright in bed. 'I'w do-ooh for ya! A-a-ah! Do-o-ooh for ya! Sh-shoo!' Philemon was squealing in a high, quavering voice, making odd tearing movements with his frail white fingers. 'I'w do-ooh for the sss-cum!' 'Vanya!' she screamed and ran over to him. His face was bright purple, his eyes shut tight. 'Vanya!' she moaned and, without thinking what she was doing, shook him by the shoulder. Philemon, purple-faced, opened his bulldog mouth, and at once his short fleshy tongue lolled out as if torn off at the root. She thrust her bare feet into a pair of rubber galoshes, tore outside as she was, bareheaded and in her flannelette nightdress, and ran gasping for breath down the pitch-black road towards the security guard's hut, which had the only telephone for the whole dacha settlement. An hour later, wheezing sibilantly and with a white sheet draped over his short body, Philemon was being loaded into an ambulance by two medical orderlies, while she, hugging her capacious sagging bosom in the flannelette nightdress, explained to them that she couldn't accompany her husband to the hospital as there was no-one else to stay with their granddaughter. Going back into the bedroom, which was filled with black silvery darkness, its window open to the thickets of jasmine outside, she sat on the disordered bed from which they had just carried the purple-faced old man, and began to weep, quietly and with restraint. Her tears were somehow unpremeditated, almost mechanical. Poor Vanya. Please God, don't let him die. A lifetime together. The phrases were imprinted readymade inside her head, as if someone had written them there in bold type: Don't let him die. Poor Vanya. A lifetime together. Alyona woke up and started howling in a deep voice. She struggled to pick the child up. 'Stop crying now. Granddad's not very well. Poor Granddad.' Alyona gave a resounding hiccup and went quiet. In the morning Tatyana came by taxi and stayed with Alyona while she hurried off to the Kremlin hospital. Philemon lay limply in bed, looking somewhat paler now, enmeshed in a network of tubes; he recognized her and struggled to move his short arm with its covering of grey hairs. She sat with him for half an hour, straightening his sheet and rubbing a warm damp towel over the bulldog face with its sparse growth of spiky bristles, then, her heart thumping, shuffled out into the corridor to waylay the doctor attending him. He reassured her that Philemon's case was not hopeless: he'd not suffered a major stroke as such, and there was every reason to hope for a recovery. It was as if a weight had been lifted from her shoulders. She stayed in the city throughout that hot July, every day making her way by trolleybus to the market and then on to the hospital, every night cooking diet soups or grating chicken liver for him, distrustful even of the Kremlin hospital and muttering to herself that you couldn't beat good home cooking. Once as she was sitting by his bedside she dozed off suddenly, and her gaunt head with the grey-dappled hair in a bun at the back nodded forwards. She dreamed she was sitting on some sort of wooden bunk, combing her hair, in a sweltering dormitory hut full of naked women. So bizarre and frightening was the dream that she woke up again immediately, moaning gently in her frail elderly voice. In front of her, ruddy-cheeked and wearing his own red pyjamas, lay Philemon, using his stubby, hirsute fingers to tuck in with obvious relish to some strawberries she had brought him. Still half-asleep, she thought he had cut himself and had blood all over his fingers, and this gave her a nasty shock. But Philemon, now almost fully recovered, suddenly winked at her with his right eye, recently operated on for a cataract, and said: 'D'you remember how I proposed to you, eh?' With a toss of her head she burst out laughing, holding her hand in front of her mouth with its fringe of black hairs. 'Well, who'd remember that?' she responded, still laughing. 'How many years ago was it? Nearly fifty! My, you've got your faculties back, and no mistake!' 'You can say that again,' said Philemon, licking sweet strawberry blood from his thumb. 'Uh-huh-huh...I'm gonna marry that dark-haired lass, I said to meself — and marry her I did! D'you remember, Zhenya?' She shook silently with tingling, blissful laughter. 'Marry her I did? You old rascal, you! Just about on the mend again, and talking like that! Lie still now! Shall I grate an apple for you? I brought the grater with me rather than do it at home so it'll be nice and fresh.' Philemon was not listening. 'Aye...' he continued. 'Marry her I did! With all the trimmings. And then I took that dark-haired lass with me, over the hills and far away. Uh-huh-huh...' She took the grater out of her bag and was about to start grating the apple for him when suddenly her head nodded forwards and she fell asleep again. And again she was surrounded by the naked women in the sweltering barracks.

More than a year went by. The dacha season was nearing its end, although the days continued hot and sunny. One Sunday morning she rose very early, heated up a pail of water and then for some reason carried it out into the dense tangle of nettles behind the shed. 'I'll wash here,' she said to herself, completely forgetting that she had her own little bathhouse, painted bright blue. Philemon had taken a steam bath in there the day before. With a bundle of birch twigs she had thrashed his hunched red back with its peppering of large pitch-black moles while he stood holding his shaggy, grey-haired stomach in with his hands, issuing orders: 'Pile on the heat, Zhenya! More steam!' 'What do you want with more steam, Vanya,' she reasoned with him as she stood there barefoot, her satin housecoat half-undone, wiping the streaming beads of sweat from her face with one forearm. 'You think about your blood pressure, never mind more steam!' 'Oh-ho-ho!' roared Philemon, his stocky frame bloated with blood, and then let his stomach out again. 'Nothing wrong with my blood pressure. Steam baths can't do us Russians anything but good!' He leaned forwards with his elbows on the bench and his back to her, so that she could beat him some more with the birch twigs and rinse off the remaining soapsuds. She suddenly felt sick at the sight of his hunched red back with its large pitch-black moles, his splayed bandy legs with their sparse covering of slicked-down hairs, the frothy wisps of lather on his buttocks... 'I feel as if I can't breathe in here, Vanya,' she mumbled. 'Dry yourself off now, and let's go and have our tea. It's time to get Alyona ready for bed...'

'Can't breathe?' said Philemon, suddenly cowed. 'How come you can't breathe? Let's get out then...' They had their tea on the veranda: she, Philemon, Tatyana and Alyona. In the garden apples fell from the branches, plummeting to the ground with a gentle hiss. Each falling apple made her jump. The low-hanging pink lampshade left behind by the dacha's previous owners cast a circle of light on the table, inside which shone glistening-wet beads of caviar, white aerated bread, and a golden-crusted apple pie, slightly burnt at the edges, which had been cut into generous slices. Tatyana's voice sounded like a duck quacking as she cajoled Alyona to drink up all her cream. The child was choking on her glass and blowing bubbles of cream. 'Oh, oh, oh!' quacked Tatyana, manoeuvring her bare bony arm to wipe Alyona's chin. 'Watch out, Grandma might come and gobble up our cream — yum! Some nasty little girl we don't know might gobble it up — yum!' Alyona started breathing heavily, like a frog, and brought up some vomit on her lace-trimmed bib. 'Oh dear, oh dear!' quavered Philemon. 'Poor little thing... Give us a cloth, Zhenya, she's been sick again...' She started running into the kitchen to get a cloth, but was suddenly transfixed with terror: even as she watched, a puffed-up creature with purple quivering cheeks was clambering on to another smaller creature with bulging eyes and an enormous green ribbon on its head which gave it the appearance of a frog. Flapping about between these two was a bare, bony fish with ribs sticking out this way and that and brittle hair standing on end. The fish was quacking stridently, opening wide its narrow, naked mouth to reveal broken fragments of white bone inside. She leaned against the door frame and screwed up her eyes. Her head had started ringing, slowly and solemnly like the tolling of an Easter bell. 'Give us a cloth, Zhenya.' The familiar voice had a menacing edge to it. 'A cloth, give us a cloth. What's up?' She opened her eyes. Sitting looking at her in the circle of light from the lampshade were Philemon, red and wrinkled from his steam bath, the anaemic-looking Tatyana with her bare collar-bones, and Alyona, huge and woebegone, gorged on a diet of sugar and fat, with pink and white vomit on her lace-trimmed bib. Suddenly remembering what she was supposed to do, she found a cloth and, trembling unaccountably with fear, handed it to Philemon. Their hands touched briefly. She imagined he was about to strike her — about to slash her wrists with something sharp and sweaty held in his hand. Hastily she backed away, smiling submissively. Tatyana picked up Alyona and ran into the kitchen to clean her up. Philemon handed the cloth back to her now it was no longer needed. 'Uh-huh-huh,' he muttered, threatening her quite openly now with a small sharp knife. 'Uh-huh-huh, Zhenya...'

That night she hardly slept. She kept getting up and going to the window to look at the slithery, overripe moon, struggling to stay up in the sky. She was too scared even to steal a glance at where Philemon lay snoring noisily. She felt that in spite of the loud snoring his green eyes were open wide in the dark, following her every move. Underneath her eiderdown she felt a little easier: it provided her with a defence, a coat of armour. Yet no sooner had she wrapped herself in it than her eyelids began to droop. No, she mustn't sleep: Philemon was just waiting for her to drop off. To do what? She really had no idea. Perhaps (she began to imagine) he wouldn't kill her at all, but on the contrary climb into her bed for a kiss and cuddle ('I said I'd marry her, and marry her I did,' she remembered), and then she'd have to lie still beneath the weight of his large hairy stomach. Or she imagined him sending her outside to stand watch over the house in place of a guard dog (she was troubled by a vague memory of something to do with a guard dog, but couldn't quite work out what it was). Or — and this was the most frightening of all — she could almost feel the touch of that small sharp knife of his with the hairs sticking to it...

As it grew light she threw on her dressing gown and began moving silently about the house. She went into their grand-daughter's room. Instead of Alyona there was a dead, swollen doll lying in the cot, pretending to be asleep. The doll didn't want to turn back into a human being, didn't want to grow, because it knew it had only a life of misfortune and ridicule to look forward to. She was shocked and felt sorry for the doll, and stroked its head with a hand dappled brown with age spots. Next she crept stealthily up the creaking stairs, stopping outside the room where Tatyana was sleeping with that fastidious, stubborn man of hers, who had come by train the previous evening. First she heard a hoarse wheezing, followed by gurgling from a woman's throat, a liquid flow that sounded like: 'arl-narl-arl-narl...' She realized that Tatyana's boy friend must be strangling her, had perhaps already killed her; yet she was too terrified to intervene and decided to stand and listen a little longer. 'Arl-narl-arl,' came the mumbling. She couldn't understand a word, although Tatyana was speaking quite loud. By contrast the boy friend's quiet responses were not only easy to make out, but for some reason lodged in her memory at once. 'One can in principle achieve physical gratification with any woman,' he said, articulating precisely, his teeth clashing together as he took a bite of something. 'Any woman, I would say, in principle. But whether one can settle down to family life with any woman is a very, very big question indeed. A question of principle, I should say.' Again he took a bite of something, and a loud quacking came from Tatyana in response. 'It's not my intention in principle to avoid the issue,' he continued. 'The time we've been together speaks for itself. And if I can be assured that my household will be run entirely in accordance with the principles laid down by me, I shall be prepared to start considering my decision as early as tomorrow.' He must have started strangling Tatyana some more, for again she uttered a hoarse gasp. 'We can in principle get married, provided such a step doesn't bring disorder and indiscipline into my life,' he said. A stream of: 'arl-narl-arl' poured from Tatyana's throat, then her boy friend said, 'Agreed,' and they both fell silent. Unable to hold back any longer, she opened the door a crack and peeped in. The long strand of hair which Tatyana's boy friend combed over his head by day to cover his bald patch now hung down to one side as he lay on her anaemic body, gently strangling her and at the same time moving rhythmically up and down. They had not noticed her intrusion and, pale blue in the light of early dawn, continued their conversation. All this aroused in her mixed feelings of fear and disgust; although deep down she recalled that at one time she herself had wished for Tatyana and this man to lie together like that at nights in the room she had scrubbed clean specially. Trying not to make too much noise breathing, she went downstairs, crawled under her eiderdown and fell fast asleep. Very soon she was awake again; jumping feverishly out of bed, she heated up a pail of water in the kitchen and went out into the dense tangle of nettles behind the shed. 'I'll wash here,' she said to herself and began hastily to undress. Removing every last stitch of clothing, she let her thinning grey-dappled hair down over her shoulders and began carefully pouring water over herself from a dark blue pitcher with white spots. The water was too cold, and her skin turned to goose-pimples all over. Then she took a bar of household soap and quickly and energetically lathered herself all over, before once again scooping water from the pail. 'Zhenya!' she heard Philemon's quavering voice call from somewhere close by. 'Zhenya! Where have you got to?' Terrified, she squatted down and pressed her head against her trembling knees. She was hidden from him by burdocks and nettles. The ground shook with approaching footsteps: Philemon was using his stick with the heavy bronze handle to poke through the grass in search of his Baucis. She crouched bow-legged on the ground, covered in a bluish-grey film of household soap, her teeth chattering with fear. She realized that he was level with the back of the shed and would catch sight of her any moment. 'Lord save and protect me!' she whispered to herself and crawled straight into the nettles, oblivious to their stinging. Squat and purple-faced, Philemon stood five paces from her, wearing his white sun hat and white nightshirt, with slippers on his bare feet. His bleary, ailing eyes could not see her. 'Zhenya!' he mumbled anxiously. 'Where on earth has she got to?' Then, taking the key from the wall, he set about unlocking the shed. She remembered that it was not really a shed at all, but a prison-camp barrack made up to look like one to stop neighbours from the other dachas asking awkward questions, and that in fact they had just arrived in Uzbekistan from Moscow for Philemon to take up his new post as commandant of the women's camp. She remembered being left behind with Larisa, who had just been born, her milk drying up during the journey to their new home, and having to heat water up in a big cast-iron tub to bath Larisa and wash herself. The house they were supposed to live in had not been finished yet, so for the time being they moved into a small dacha, leaving all their suitcases piled up in one corner. Having already seen to it that the man responsible for their reception and accommodation was hauled over the coals in appropriate fashion, Philemon told her she'd have to make do for a few more days. They had arrived the day before, she worn down by the wailing of her hungry daughter and one of the migraines which would suddenly overtake her and then drag on for weeks on end. They were met at the station and taken to the house of a fat Uzbek who looked for all the world as if his layers of fat had been trussed round and round with invisible threads. Here they were invited to sit on feather mattresses laid out on the floor and were served rich pilaff, wine and hot tea, while the Uzbek smiled a smile like a recumbent moon, the medals on his chest jingling urgently. 'Aye,' Philemon said to her, stretching his bulldog jaw in a yawn as he got into bed. 'Aye... I'll sort this lot out. Think they can run rings round us...'

He stood there a little longer, poking about with his stick. Then he took off his sun hat and wiped his eyes with it. She had never seen him cry before. 'Zhenya,' he sobbed, 'where are you? Don't frighten me like this.' His chin started quivering slightly. She just knew he was putting on an act to make her come out of the nettles. 'Oh no, you can forget that,' she muttered to herself. 'You can just stew for a bit longer...' Philemon turned round and, sobbing, went back to the house to wake up Tatyana and her boy friend. Meanwhile, keeping her head down, she crawled to a section of the fence with a large hole covered with sheets of plywood. Here she made her break for freedom into the forest of fir trees which began just the other side of the fence.

'No-one's going to escape from my camp!' said Philemon, bringing his hairy hand down hard on the table. 'There are no forests here, nowhere to hide! You'd better be sure they're back here again by tomorrow!' She nodded approvingly as she washed the dishes. Philemon was tearing strips off a pimply man in uniform standing in front of him while, scalding his mouth, he ate the borscht she had prepared. Good, thick, blood-red borscht it was, with specks of yellow fat swimming in it. The man in uniform stared at the plate with a sullen, hounded look in his eyes. 'Got that?' wheezed Philemon, knocking back a glassful and taking a deep breath as if surfacing from the bottom of a river. 'That's all, you can go.' She dried her hands on a clean towel and sat down next to him. 'Who's escaped then, Vanya?' 'Two of those bitches. One Jewish, the other Russian. Yesterday, it was. We'll catch 'em again, and then, you see, I'll give 'em what's what! They won't forget me in a hurry!' His clear blue, bulging eyes had turned bloodshot. 'No sirree!' The baby started crying in the next room. She went in, then came back again. 'Have you seen our little toothy-woothy?' she crooned. 'Lala's second tooth is coming through!' 'Hm... Damn me!' Philemon grunted approvingly, patting her on the arm. 'A tooth, eh? Let's take a look...' They stood over the cot, admiring the little squirrel tooth in the infant's mouth. 'Damn me,' Philemon repeated, and then frowned. 'You know, one of those sluts that got away is pregnant. Six months gone, so they tell me.' 'No!' she gasped in disbelief. 'She couldn't even care less about her baby, then? Risking her own life like that, and never mind the baby — what sort of a mother is that?' 'Come on, Zhenya, let's go for a spin,' yawned Philemon. 'Wrap our little girl up well. We'll get a breath of fresh air.' He sat in front next to the driver, she in the back. The whole steppe was ablaze with dark-red poppies. 'Damn me,' he said, turning round to her with a grin across the width of his jaw. 'Remember in the royal box at the Bolshoi? Looks the same sort of colour...' That night he heaved his hirsute, well-fed belly on top of her. Compliantly, anxious that he might no longer find her attractive, she panted with feigned pleasure. 'My dark-haired little beauty,' he grunted as he was dropping off to sleep a few minutes later. 'Damn me... I'll kill those bitches, you mark my words. Hang 'em from the nearest tree. Think they can run rings round us...'

It was getting on for midday by the time they found her and brought her home. She came out of the forest without protest, her naked body covered in crimson nettle stings, her large work-flattened hands hanging inertly at her sides. Tatyana's boy friend and a freckle-faced policeman stood either side of her, guiding her uncertainly towards the garden gate. With a frown on his face, the policeman moved awkwardly as he tried somehow to shield her from view, although as luck would have it the only person in the lane at that moment was Tatyana, leaning pallidly against the fence. At the sight of her mother she began shaking as if in a fever, and started to take her jacket off. 'Right, then,' said the policeman, frowning and looking away from Tatyana. 'It seems fairly clear to me that what's needed here is medical assistance. A mental home, or something of that sort. There's nothing we can do to help.' 'Oh, Mummy,' breathed Tatyana, her lips quivering uncontrollably. 'Why, why?' 'It's a waste of time, in principle, asking pointless questions,' said her boy friend, articulating precisely. He bridled with anger. 'We have to get her inside the house.' She heard what he had said and tossed her head. 'I'll go by myself,' she mumbled. 'It's time for lunch, I'll go myself...' She climbed the veranda steps, supported by Tatyana, and saw in the doorway the portly, panic-stricken figure of Philemon. At the sight of his naked, dishevelled Baucis, her whole body a mass of red blotches, he began to back away from her, cringing and covering his face with his hairy hands. Baucis was choked with fear, and would have fallen if Tatyana and her boy friend had not caught her in time. 'Dad!' Tatyana screamed hysterically. 'Get her something to put on! Anything! She can't walk around like this!' 'Yes, of course, of course,' said Philemon. Still cringing and backing away, he cast around for a garment of some sort. 'What on earth's the matter with her?' He grabbed an old raincoat from the coat rack and handed it gingerly to his daughter, afraid of touching the old woman's naked body. Tatyana's hands were shaking as she slipped the raincoat over her mother. 'What are we going to do?' she asked tearfully. 'She'll have to be taken away,' said Philemon, trembling fearfully. 'What else can we do? She needs proper medical attention. The doctors know best... Proper medical attention... Otherwise, who knows... She's not well, is our grandma... Bad business all round...' Suddenly Baucis fell to her knees in front of Tatyana before the boy friend could catch her. 'I'll be your servant,' she pleaded, 'I'll wash your feet. Don't send me away.' 'Oh, Mummy!' Tatyana sobbed uncontrollably. 'Oh, my God! Come inside and lie down, have a sleep. Oh, Mummy!'

Her teeth chattering, she went inside and lay down in bed without taking the raincoat off. 'All right, I'll have a sleep,' she mumbled. 'What a to-do... Have a sleep...'

Philemon was crying and wiping the tears from his quivering bulldog cheeks with his grey-haired fists. 'At least take me back to town, then,' he begged Tatyana. 'Or you, Boris, give me a lift into Moscow, there's a good chap. I can't stay in the same house as a mental case. Just looking at her could send my blood pressure shooting up.' Tatyana had regained her composure. 'We mustn't rush into anything, Dad,' she said reasonably. 'Let's keep an eye on her for a couple of days. I'll be here anyway, and Boris is staying today and tomorrow. I feel sorry for her. It could just be some age-related condition that'll go away again.' 'That is in principle quite feasible,' her boy friend confirmed. 'I heard of a colleague in our department who experienced a similar episode with his aunt which in principle had no lasting effects...'

## II

'Perhaps I could stay at home, Vanya?' she whispered in her sleep. 'The children are poorly, and I don't feel...' 'No, you can't.' replied Philemon. 'You have to be at the concert. All the top brass'll be there. And don't you dare show me up.' They sat in the front row of the packed hall. On the stage, which was decked out with flags and flowers, stood three rows of women in white hospital robes. She remembered as she slept how proud Philemon had been of this idea, which he had thought up himself: a week before the concert sixty new hospital gowns had been delivered to the camp. Now these dead women in their clean white burial linen, flinging open mouths full of rotting teeth, sang at full pitch: '...our tanks are swift as lightning...' Philemon wrinkled his brow with pleasure, although the lower half of his face retained its usual fierce expression. Their song finished, on the word of command the dead women executed a left turn and shuffled off stage in their felt hospital slippers. The audience applauded. Then three women who had not taken part in the singing appeared on stage, dressed in the same white gowns and with large wreaths of poppies on their heads, which made it look as if flames were leaping from their hair. They presented the visiting V.I.P. with an enormous embroidered cushion which had, worked in red silk in the middle of it, the promise: 'Through honest toil on behalf of the Motherland we shall earn the forgiveness of Party and People!' In her dream she could not make out the figure that had accompanied Philemon up the steps. She had only a sense of the word 'V.I.P.' itself, and gradually she began to feel that Philemon's hairy fingers were supporting something rough-textured and dark in creaking boots, something that had neither body nor face. As the V.I.P. extended a hand of sorts to accept the gift of the cushion, one of the dead women with red fire in their hair spat in his face. 'Bastard!' she screamed as they hurriedly dragged her away, hitting her as they went, 'Bastard!' They stopped the dead woman's mouth, yet still she managed to call out through blood and sputum: 'Go to hell, the lot of you! Bastards!'

Philemon was a fearsome sight as he sat next to her in the front row, waiting for the concert to end. Stony-faced and unmoving, no longer applauding, no longer wrinkling his brow, he sat quietly grinding his teeth. Eventually he turned his unseeing eyes on her. 'You can go home on your own. You won't be needed at the supper.' 'What about you?' she asked, snuggling into the raincoat Tatyana had draped over her naked, nettle-stung body. 'Me?' Philemon retorted, clenching his knotted, black-haired fist. 'I've got things to see to.'

There was a pleasant, appetising smell of pilaff, wine and fresh bread in the house. The old Uzbek woman, one of the locals, bowed and told her in a whisper that the children had gone to sleep a long time ago. She slipped off the irksome raincoat and let it fall to the carpet, then stretched out on the bed and closed her eyes. Philemon came back in the middle of the night. An acrid, suffocating smell of sweat hung about him. 'Well?' she asked, sitting up on the feather mattress. 'Have they found Alyona?' 'I'm having her shot,' Philemon replied, his heavy jaw gaping in a yawn. 'Sabotage on behalf of foreign intelligence. Enemy operation carried out on camp territory. Think they can run rings round us...' He stood his shiny new boots against the wall and scratched his stomach beneath his shirt. 'They won't forget me in a hurry, no sirree...'

'You let me know just as soon as she wakes up,' Philemon mumbled faint-heartedly, hiding behind the large blue teapot with the red flower pattern. 'I can't even bear looking at her... Not until we've made sure... No way... It's not like a normal illness... Can't even live out my last years in peace... What sort of life is that?'

Tatyana went in and bent over her. Tatyana was wearing a white hospital gown. The poppies in her hair had long since withered and turned black. As she leaned forwards a smell of pilaff and fresh bread wafted across from her body. 'Mummy, are you feeling better?' said Tatyana. 'Where's Alyona, then?' she asked with sudden guile, remembering the name of that little woman with the ribbon in her hair. 'It's time for her afternoon tea. Tell them to pick some berries for her.' The word 'berries' made her feel slightly queasy, but she overcame this without letting on to Tatyana. 'Tell them to pick some berries, otherwise I'm going to put in a complaint against the lot of you. And I know where I can go to do it, too, thank God — it's not as though we're living in the desert here. You're starving that child to death...' With an anxious sigh Tatyana went back out on the veranda. Philemon and her boy friend looked at her. 'She's a bit better,' Tatyana said doubtfully. 'She's had a sleep and seems a bit more like her old self.' 'It all takes time,' her boy friend concurred. 'Of course, we won't leave you on your own with someone who's mentally deranged. Although it'll mean putting ourselves out quite a bit, in principle...'

She woke in the night and realized that this was the last night before their wedding. Tomorrow they were going to be married. He'd got a strong pair of hands on him: like iron, they were. When he'd grabbed her breasts a few days ago the pain had taken her breath away. Well, he was a man, wasn't he? They were all the same. At least she'd feel secure with him — he'd look after her properly. The pain you could put up with. His mother and sister lived out in the sticks somewhere, but he'd made his own way in the world, got himself educated. Salt of the earth, his kind were — the backbone of Soviet power. Everything they'd struggled to achieve depended on people like him. Anyway, you couldn't just pull away from him when he had hold of your breast, could you? She laughed out loud in the darkness. For a while she sat there thinking, then suddenly knew what she had to do. First thing tomorrow he'd have his yoghourt. He always had his yoghourt with blackcurrants, every morning. That was before breakfast. Then they'd have their breakfast together. Feeding Alyona would be a joint effort, both of them sharing titbits with her and telling her nursery rhymes and fairy-tales until they were blue in the face.

Best to put it in his yoghourt, she thought. I'll do it now; nobody'll guess. And then there'll be no wedding. It'll all be over by the time Tatyana and Alyona wake up. I'll have the breakfast ready on the table and tell them he's gone. Gone where? How should I know, just gone, that's all. My breast still hurts now. Just shows how rough he can be. That's not to say we haven't had a good life together — nobody could wish for better. All the same, I've got to do it. I'm afraid of him: that's why, that's the main reason. He'll come and grab hold of me again, strip me naked in the night and roll on top of me. And then it'll be morning sickness and having babies all over again. That's what I'm afraid of.

Trying not to let the door creak, she went out on the veranda, which was bathed in gentle light from the overripe moon. She picked up a thin glass dish for serving jam, then a hammer from the porch and went out on to the steps. There she smashed the dish with the hammer. Nobody had heard. He was asleep. Good. Surreptitiously she set about pounding the dish with the hammer, trying to grind up the broken splinters of glass. This was a method favoured by the Uzbeks. It was clean and simple. Once you started bleeding from the stomach you'd had it. She scooped up the pieces of ground glass and returned to the veranda with them held tight in her fist. Opening the door of their generously stocked refrigerator, she scattered the tiny fragments in the butter dish and replaced the lid. Then she wiped her hands, changing the towel by the washbasin while she was at it (Tatyana and her slovenly ways again!) and went back into the room. He was not there: his bed, neatly made beneath its silk cover, dimly registered empty. She snuggled down under the eiderdown and went to sleep.

'He's such a wonderful father!' she trilled to her mother as she unwrapped the presents. Her mother's eyes shone greedily, and her hands were shaking; in her whole manner there was something cowed, craven and insincere. As a child she had always been sick with fear of her mother, and since reaching adulthood had never once sought her advice or confided in her. 'He'll do anything for the children, anything! Tatyana wants to take up ballet, and any other father would have told her to forget it — you know the sort of thing: "You a ballerina? You can drop those fancy ideas!" But not him! He said: "Fine, if that's what you want, we'll get you into the Bolshoi ballet school, and you can dance to your heart's content." He'd do anything for them!' Her mother's hands trembled as she snatched a length of grey gaberdine. 'Is this for me, too?' she asked, flashing the same false lopsided smile her daughter assumed whenever she wanted to make a pleasing remark to someone. 'It's all for you, all from him! "We've got to do her proud," he said. He chose it all himself: shoes, winter clothes, everything! "For Nina Timofeyevna, with regards from her devoted son-in-law," — those were his actual words. Ha, ha! You see what sort of a man he is?' 'Of course, Zhenya, of course,' her mother replied with a toss of her mobile head. 'We know what sort of posting you were on... Very demanding work, I should imagine. They won't take just anyone for that, only people of the highest calibre, people of spotless character. Oh yes, we know about that. But what's the climate like there, the weather?' 'Very hot, Mummy. Almost too hot in summer. But we had this marvellous house there, with two verandas, and our own orchard. And in spring it's so beautiful, it really hits you in the face. Poppies everywhere — all the desert and the hills ablaze with them. Just incredible. I stayed at home with the children. We had a nanny, a woman came every other day to do the cleaning, and another one came to cook for us, all local people. We used to drive into town for concerts or the theatre — we had our own chauffeur-driven car. I tell you, we had everything.' There was an envious whistle from her mother's thin pimply throat. 'Well I never! You know, people used to ask me, "How's your daughter coping in a place like that after living in Moscow?" I'd say, "Great, everything's fine," but on the inside I'd be worried sick about you myself. After all, you were there on your own with two children, and I suppose Vanya was tied up with his work all day.' 'He was, all day. After all, we were dealing with criminals, and you had no time to think about yourself. Awful types, they were, enemies of the people. But Vanya was always humane — never treated them unfairly, always went by the book. After all, they were human beings too, and they'd been sent to us to be reformed. We hoped the voice of conscience might be awakened in them. We did what we could.'

Small and waxen-looking, Philemon knocked at the door of Tatyana's bedroom. She came to the door in a frilly nylon nightdress, still half asleep. 'What are you doing up, Dad? You're driving me round the bend, the pair of you!' 'I know, I know,' he mumbled. 'But I really would like to get back to town. I haven't been able to sleep a wink, I'm so scared. I've never had anything to do with mentally abnormal people before, never in my whole life. Gangsters and criminals, yes, but at least they were sane. Only here I haven't been able to sleep a wink.' 'My God!' Tatyana exploded. 'If only you could hear yourself! It's not as if we're talking about some stranger here, is it? Think of all the years you've been together!' 'Who's interested in that now?' Philemon quavered, shifting from one foot to the other in his large tan-coloured slippers. 'All right, we've been together, been through all sorts — but why should I be expected to sacrifice what's left of my life now for the sake of her illness? I didn't shed my blood for that, I can tell you... Always up there in the thick of it. Yes, we stayed together all these years — God only knows how...' Tatyana was aghast. 'Have you started raving now, or what? Dad! Don't you at least feel sorry for her? Just take a look at her!' 'I do, of course I do, I do feel sorry,' Philemon rattled off in one breath. 'Nobody's ever felt sorry for me, though, never in my whole life. I've always been there for others — for you and the family. Surely now I'm entitled to take things easy a bit. She could be planning to cut my throat — who knows what a crazy person might take it into their head to do?' Tatyana reeled in disbelief. 'Cut your throat? You've only to touch her and she'd fall over!' 'Yes, cut my throat,' Philemon mumbled, blowing hot breath into her face from his bulldog mouth. 'I had a dream that she was going to do just that. You can never tell what's going on inside someone else's head. It's a nightmare! Take me back to town, away from here!' 'Stop pestering me!' Tatyana hissed. 'Waking me up in the middle of the night like that!' And she slammed the door in his face. Her boy friend raised his head from the pillows, the long strand of hair hanging down from his bald patch. 'This is a madhouse, if you think about it! And if you lot think I can cope with this on top of my work load... I'm sorry, I shall be forced to take appropriate action...'

She heard them moving about somewhere, going up and down the stairs, whispering. Excellent: now they'd be afraid of her. What sort of a deal was that anyway, loading all the work on to one person? Fetching water, looking after the children... And then in the evening she had to go to the Bolshoi. Comrade Stalin himself was to be there, and they were all going to sit in the royal box. But just before the ballet, would you believe it, Philemon found he had a sty. He literally howled with rage. 'Vanya,' she told him, 'Vanya, it's not a crime! It could happen to anyone.' He very nearly let fly at her with his fists. 'What the bloody hell do you know about it! I can't let Comrade Stalin see me looking like this!' They smeared some egg white over the sty and powdered it so it wouldn't show. Even so his eye stood out like a car headlight. She didn't like jewellery, but he told her to wear a necklace, and she didn't argue. Let him have it his way. A white necklace to go with her crimson dress. Where had he got it from? He didn't say. There was a strange smell to the necklace. The smell of someone's body, or of some sort of wood, she couldn't tell which.

'How come you've got a moustache?' Philemon shouted at her in a sudden rage. 'What are you, a man or a woman?' She looked in the mirror: he was right, she had a moustache. Two hairs here, another one there... How had they grown? She hadn't noticed. She plucked them out with a pair of tweezers. When

Comrade Stalin came into the box they all stood up. Philemon's eye with the powdered sty filled with tears, and his chin trembled. Men can have feelings too, you know. What could you say against him? He was a caring father and husband... 'Caring' was putting it mildly, in fact: although he wasn't one to spoil the children, he put everything back into the house and family, and he'd never as much as looked at another woman.

'Don't expect me back tonight,' said Philemon. 'I've got to go on a tour of inspection round the camps. There've been reports of trouble there — breaches of discipline.' And off he went. The house felt comfortable and clean and smelled of bread and wine. That night it was stiflingly hot, and she threw everything off, even the sheet. She felt at peace, free to be herself. No fingers groping at her body, no-one snoring against her neck. He came back three days later in a buoyant mood, although his face looked tired and haggard. After his meal he fell into bed without even touching her.

The following day he disappeared without trace again. It was the same story the day after that. Each time he came back looking haggard, in a buoyant, truculent mood, and treated her and the children as if they weren't there. When she washed one of his shirts, she found it covered in hairs. It was a woman's hair: fair, like gossamer. She said nothing, just pretended that was how it had to be. He was a man: they were all the same. At least this was the first time he'd gone astray. Otherwise it was all work and family. Let him think he was cock of the walk, he'd be sweeter-tempered for it. Although, of course, her heart ached unbearably. She took it in her hands, squeezed it and wrung it out, twisting it like a rag; not a tear fell. Let him. He wouldn't leave her. There was Larisa, Tatyana. Would he chuck them all over for some prison-camp floosie? She never did find out whose hair it was. For a couple of months he kept coming home late and never touched her. Well, she didn't mind that, it gave her body a rest. Eventually he half-heartedly heaved himself on to her again without so much as a word. Gradually things got back to normal, just like before. There was no point trying to change men, was there?

We'll go to the market, she thought, we'll buy some rhubarb for Alyona, some rhubarb for you and some for me. What does Alyona want with rhubarb? Why, what do you mean? She may be just a child now, but when she grows up she'll have her share of tummy trouble too. We can put the rhubarb by until it's needed. Such a big lass she's turned out — there'll be boys chasing after her before we know it. Uh-huh-huh... I can't make that Boris out. If he marries Tatyana, well and good, but it'll be even better if he doesn't. That's just between you and me, though. I feel really sorry for Tatyana. She only makes out she's so hard. Actually she's got a weak heart. She had a late delivery and lost a lot of blood, so they gave her a Caesarean. And she's scared of that Boris, dead scared. He can go for weeks on end without even ringing her. Tied up in his work, he is. Of course, in his job you can't really relax or let your hair down much. Even so, he could think about his child, you can't leave it all to one person. It's only now that Philemon's come over all considerate like that: 'Zhenya, Zhenya, let's hire a maid, why do it all yourself?' In the old days he'd rant and rave: 'Get off your backside! What d'you think you are, a lady of leisure? We wiped all their sort out years ago!' She never said anything, never answered back. After all, people said that Buldayev had hanged his wife with his own hands — got fed up with her and hanged her, just like that. He was such a big shot that no-one dared speak up. They put it out as suicide caused by a brain disorder, said she just couldn't cope with things any more. Maybe that's how it was. Even so there were all sorts of rumours going round. Philemon had once yelled at her in a rage, too: 'I'll strangle you with my bare hands!' Of course, she'd just laughed... He was a man, wasn't he. They were all the same, all had to be cock of the walk.

'But you were going to stay today,' Tatyana pleaded with him. 'You've got some days off, haven't you...' Noisily her boy friend sucked coffee into his long thin throat. 'I can't manage today. In principle, I've got a full schedule all this week. But if there's any problem... I'll await further developments... Of course, if there's any problem... I'll send a car.' 'I'm sorry things have turned out like this, Boris darling,' said Tatyana with a quiver of her father's bulldog chin. 'They're old people...' 'Yes,' he agreed, 'it's a nasty business, is old age. If only they could come up with some drug or other... It'd make things a lot easier, in principle. Where is she, in the living room?' 'She's still asleep,' Tatyana sighed. 'I decided not to go in just yet. Dad's sleeping too: he took a sedative.' 'Why couldn't he sleep last night?' muttered her boy friend, sucking in more coffee. 'Was he scared, or what?' 'Don't even ask!' Tatyana replied gloomily. Red streaky blotches began to spread over her pallid skin. 'When I think of the mess they've got themselves into! And just think how they used to be: utterly devoted, in perfect harmony, always trying to please one another, never an unkind word.' 'Yes,' her boy friend agreed again. 'If only everyone could live like that. What you might call the perfect couple.'

At this point she shuffled out of the bedroom, taking short little steps and cringing, a fawning smile on her face. Instead of the raincoat she was now wearing a dress with a white collar which she kept for special occasions. Why on earth had they brought a dress like that to the dacha? They couldn't have been thinking. Anyway, it had come in useful now. She had not got round to combing her hair, which hung loose and grey-dappled over her shoulders, but she had managed to put her shoes on. 'Mummy!' Tatyana wailed. 'Why are you saying "Mummy" like that?' she smiled, concealing her fear. 'I've been your Mummy for forty years now! Ha, ha! I had a nice little sleep, and then I thought it's about time I got on with my work. Otherwise you could sleep your whole life away. Have you cooked today's dinner yet?' Tatyana and her boy friend exchanged glances. Taking her time, she sat at the table and poured herself a cup of tea with shaking hands. They mustn't realize how scared she was, that was the main thing. Really she ought to ask if he was still alive. She smiled even more fulsomely: 'Don't say you're planning to desert us, Boris? What a shame... Such lovely weather.. You could have gone down to the river for a spot of fishing.' The word "river" made her feel queasy too. It was the water: they'd throw the body in there at night, under cover of darkness, and what proof would there be then? She took a sip of tea and frowned: it tasted like dishwater. She'd have to make some stewed fruit. Plenty of rhubarb, with blackcurrants and nettles. Nice and tart, and thick enough for a spoon to stand up in. Otherwise, what with Tatyana being such a bad cook, he might not marry her. Tatyana's boy friend gave an indecisive cough. 'Well, as far as I can see, in principle, there's no fundamental danger any more. I can leave you here without any qualms.' Hastily adjusting his wayward strand of hair and licking off a grain of caviar which had stuck to his lip, he snatched up his briefcase and was out of the garden gate and gone before they knew it. 'I'll go and pick some mushrooms in the forest for Alyona,' she lied. 'Or wild strawberries. I've always said, Tanya, haven't I, there's nothing to beat our wild strawberries straight from the forest. The taste, the aroma — there's nothing else to compare. And packed with vitamins.' Tatyana just managed to contain herself. 'Don't go, Mummy,' she said. 'Look, you're all shaky, and anyway, you're not quite... Listen to me, don't go!' I ought to ask her, she thought, ask if he's still alive. Otherwise what's the point of hiding? Perhaps they've even buried him already? If so, I'll take this dress off, and the shoes, and we'll cook the dinner. But what if he's alive? No, I don't want to risk it. It's only when you're young you get a thrill from taking risks. But at our time of life, uh-huh-huh... She pushed her cup aside. 'Don't be silly, Tanya,' she said reasonably. I brought you and Larisa up, I've nursed Alyona for you — what makes you suddenly think I'm soft in the head? Can't I go for a walk in the forest?' And off she went, down the steps of the veranda, numb with terror because she had to turn her back on the locked door to his bedroom. Passing a blackcurrant bush, she flicked a maggot off one of the branches (they'd eaten all the berries, there was nothing left to give Alyona!) At the gate she turned round; he was standing in the doorway, looking at her. His mouth open, his eyes bleary (they'd forgotten his drops!), he stood there barefoot in his white nightshirt. She wondered whether he'd come running after her or not. How could he, though? His legs were all knotted and stiff; she'd have no problem getting away. So why not have a bit of fun now, she thought: I'll wave to him and call out, 'Hello Vanya! Good morning to you!' She waved to him, her fingers trembling. 'Where's she off to?' Philemon croaked hoarsely, clutching hold of Tatyana's shoulder. 'Where's she going?' 'For a walk,' Tatyana said quietly. 'She wants to pick some berries. She's feeling better.' 'Tanya, please,' Philemon snivelled, 'you're the only person I can turn to. Get me away from here, there's a good girl!' 'I've told you, she's feeling better! She's gone for a walk. Now come and have your breakfast.'

Two hours later Tatyana and two sympathetic women from neighbouring dachas set out to look for her. They searched the whole forest but saw no sign of her. Tatyana ran to the police station, and it was the same story all over again. She was found among some aspen trees and led home, clasping her hands to her heart and protesting her innocence: 'What's all the fuss about? My God, can't I even go for a walk? The doctor told me to get plenty of fresh forest air.' The other women just shrugged their shoulders and said,

'Look at her, Tanya: perhaps there is nothing wrong with her after all? She's probably just tired of slaving away in the kitchen all day and wants a bit of a rest.' 'What are you getting so worked up about? That's exactly what I've been saying!' she laughed. 'Not even allowed to get a breath of fresh air! All my life I've been at their beck and call. At least now in my old age you'd think I'd be entitled to do what I want. I am entitled to go for a walk, am I?' Tatyana's pupils were contracting and dilating in turn as she looked at her mother. 'Are you having me on, or what? What's wrong with you?' 'Can't you understand plain language?' she snapped back, waving her arms. 'There's nothing wrong with me! I'm tired of slaving away in the kitchen, and anyone would tell you the same! Just let me get a bit of fresh air!' Tatyana broke down in tears. 'Mummy, don't do this to me! My head's spinning! Are you all right again or not?'

Good job she's thick, she won't cotton on. Let her think I want to go for a walk. Always a bit short in the brains department, she was. Oh, bright enough at book-learning, but worse than a child when it comes to real life. Shouldn't be too hard pulling the wool over her eyes. All I need is for her to leave, so I'm left on my own with him. I'll bury him myself, too. If you want a job done properly, you've got to do it yourself, and that's a fact. It's kill or be killed. They wouldn't let me escape, so it's the only way. Not that I'm not scared, of course. Still, it'll be the very last time. Just this little bit more fear, and then I'll be free.

'No way!' Philemon chortled. 'Trying to shack me up with your niece! You should see my woman: phoarr, real stunner, she is! I've been on cloud nine ever since we got married. Total respect, she's got: she'll wash my feet if I tell her to. No, you'll have to go a long way to find a woman like mine. She'll be here in a week or so, then we'll invite you over and you can see for yourself. I tell you, she's a right scorcher!' 'What's her name?' asked the man in the military-style jacket worn unbuttoned at the chest as he filled their glasses with cold transparent vodka. 'Tell me your woman's name, and we'll drink a toast to her.' 'Zhenya!' Philemon croaked tenderly. 'Dark-haired lass, she is, like a little cat, but well-built with it.' 'Well, you've certainly got it bad,' said the other with a sardonic grin. 'Never known you to go all soft like that...' 'What d'you mean, soft?' said Philemon with a look of surprise, emptying his glass in one. 'Soft, you say... We can't afford to be soft in our line of work. I've seen enough women in my time, as you well know. Spent five years looking at 'em as commandant. Saw 'em naked and all sorts. They were obliged to wash in my presence if I demanded it, yes sirree! All part of the discipline! After all, I was supposed to be like a doctor — curing the bitches, rehabilitating them.' 'Well, and...' asked his friend with a sly look. 'Did they — as part of the discipline?' 'What do you think? Of course they did! Washed and dried themselves without so much as a squeak.' 'You're going to miss that job!' 'Oh no, I've had enough of it now,' Philemon frowned. 'There's more important things to do in the world. When the Party commands, it's my duty to go without question. As for Zhenya, she'll go with me like a mare with her master. I'll take her by the reins, and she'll come trotting along behind. Yes sirree...'

I won't be able to manage him on my own, there's no way I will. What a mess. You see, that's just an act he's putting on all the time — pretending to be old and ill like that. He's not old at all. If he didn't die then, he never will. He'll just go on tormenting me. He'll make me wash his feet. I'll bath Alyona first, then wash his feet in the same water (no point heating up a new lot, is there?) That glass didn't work after all — I couldn't have ground up enough. Too late now, though — they've hidden the hammer, and the glass dishes too. It's time I was off. People used to live in the forests, good Lord they did — whole families, with children! I'll get settled in first, and then Alyona and Tatyana can move in with me. My little daughters, that I brought into the world and raised. As soon as I'm settled in I'll get them away from him, otherwise he's bound to put them in that prison-camp hut. 'Get working!' he'll say. 'Think you can run rings round me, do you... There'll be no theatre for you, none of that ballet stuff.'

Quietly she pulled on her dress, then removed the pillowcase from her pillow and slipped into it a pair of rubber galoshes, a loaf of bread and a piece of soap in its holder. That should do, she thought, it's only to tide me over for now. Folk'll help me out when I get there. Of course, there are no forests here, but there'll be poppies growing thicker than any forest. I'll hide in among them and decide what to do then. The Uzbeks like us. The way they lived here before Soviet power — like the Stone Age, it was! She walked down the steps, steadying herself on the handrail. Moonlight crept over her face. The sky was turning grey in anticipation of dawn. Suddenly she decided she wanted to give Alyona a kiss. She set the pillowcase down on the steps and without a sound went back into the living room. Alyona was nowhere to be seen. She tried to remember which room she might be sleeping in and became confused. He was in the room off this one, Tatyana was upstairs. So where was Alyona? She couldn't be with him, could she? Oh God, oh God! She started crossing herself, making little signs of the cross on her chest with unpractised fingers. That was just an act he was putting on, for heaven's sake! How come Tatyana didn't realize? She stood in the darkness, shifting from one foot to the other. Well, it would have to wait for another time. Now it was goodbye.

glas